D1346377

Design for Murder

Design for Murder

Roy Lewis

ROBERT HALE · LONDON

© Roy Lewis 2010
First published in Great Britain 2010

ISBN 978-0-7090-8969-8

Robert Hale Limited
Clerkenwell House
Clerkenwell Green
London EC1R 0HT

www.halebooks.com

The right of Roy Lewis to be identified as
author of this work has been asserted by him
in accordance with the Copyright, Designs and
Patents Act 1988

2 4 6 8 10 9 7 5 3 1

MORAY COUNCIL LIBRARIES & INFO.SERVICES	
20 28 09 20	
Askews	
MF	

Typeset in 11¾/15½pt Palatino
by Derek Doyle & Associates, Shaw Heath
Printed in Great Britain by the MPG Books Group, Bodmin and King's Lynn

PROLOGUE

The woman had stopped screaming.

It was too soon. He straightened, stared at her. His long, loose, smock-like shirt was soaked with excited sweat, stained with blood, his eyes were stinging, and his whole body was trembling, tingling angrily with anticipation.

For she had fainted. The frustration began to boil in him. He laid aside the scalpel after wiping it on the towel and sat back in the chair he had drawn up in front of his victim. He stared at her naked body. Her head had slumped forward, tangled blonde hair hanging down, obscuring her face, but with her hands bound behind the chair back her body remained upright. He watched the slow rivulet of blood coursing down from her breasts, marking a dark, slippery trail towards her navel, congealing, encrusting at its edges, pooling between her thighs.

He shuddered. It was far too soon. He was not ready. He had not yet finished the design, the completion of which would allow him release, satisfaction, and a final sexual explosion. He glared around the dim cellar: his workplace. The subject slumped before him was brightly lit by the arc lamp that he had installed to one side, but the rest of the cellar was shadowed, dark-cornered, a reflection, he thought grimly to himself, of the corners of his mind. Because he held few illusions about himself: then compulsion was all.

He sighed, shook himself like an animal throwing off water from its coat. It was no good if she was not awake, responsive, talking, begging, screaming. But this was the third time she had lost consciousness and the bottle of smelling salts was empty. Moreover, he became aware of the slow gnawing in his stomach, the hunger for alcohol that sometimes came to him in the middle of his work. It was not welcome, and it damaged his concentration, but it happened. He would have to stop his task for a while, leave the woman alone in the dark, damp cellar.

He rose, made a careful inspection of his handiwork, the neat cutting of Libra, the Scales, clucking his tongue with disappointment at being unable to continue the careful slicing of the flesh. He moved away, stripping off the stained shirt, washed his chest, hands and upper arms in the stone sink that was located in the corner of the room, shuddering at the coldness of the water. He moved across to the glowing electric heater, stood in front of it as he dried himself, wiped the sweat from his forehead. He slipped on a roll-neck sweater, shrugged into the heavy jacket hanging on the wall. He buttoned it up to his throat. He took considerable care locking the cellar door with the heavy new padlock he had bought in the supermarket, climbed the rickety stairs and shivered as he crossed the long concrete floor of the dark, empty, echoing warehouse.

In the street outside the wind was cold, cutting across the empty road, causing the street lamps to flicker, and whirling, discarded newspapers whipped and danced against his legs. To his left the dilapidated quayside, soon destined to be redeveloped into a luxury housing project if the journals were to be believed, lay deserted, with black, debris-littered water lapping against decayed timbers and rusting iron.

It was half a mile to the nearest pub.

The interior of the Coach and Horses sent a gust of stale, warm odorous air into his face as he thrust his way into the bar. He unbuttoned the top of his jacket, leaned on the counter, and ordered a whisky and a ham sandwich from the barman, who nodded to him in vague recognition. They never spoke beyond the brief ordering. When the sandwich was placed in front of him, with the whisky, he checked his watch. It would be an hour or so before the chemist shop in the shopping centre would be closing: he had time to relax for a while before making the necessary purchase and returning to his task.

He glanced around the bar. Among the various people present there were a few faces he recognized as regulars – a group of grubby-jeaned workers from the local building site celebrating the end of their shift, and a couple of businessmen taking refreshment before going home to their boring wives. He never engaged in conversation with them: they had their lives and he had his. He smiled slightly as he imagined what they might think of his cellar activities.

He would have liked to take off his jacket because the room was warm but he was reluctant to do so. He could not be certain he had washed away all the bloodstains. He glanced at his hands, but they were clean except for some dark encrustations under his nails. He munched on his sandwich, sipped the whisky, picked casually at his nails, cleaning them.

There were two young women seated in the far corner of the bar. One of them looked familiar. He thought he might have seen her in the Coach and Horses on other occasions. As he stared at them the woman's companion rose, kissed her lightly on the cheek, and slipped into her coat before making her way from the bar into the cold street outside. He watched her go, then as the door swung behind her his glance switched back to the girl who stayed.

Her eyes met his briefly; he thought he detected a slight smile on her lips. Her face was a pale oval and her dark hair was cut short. There was the promise of a full body, swelling breasts under the dark business jacket she wore, and her legs were long, he guessed. He began to create fantasies about that body, guessing at its contours, the hollows and the swellings, the softness and the possibilities it could offer for his skills.

His mind snapped back to reality. He already had a work in hand. This was no time to be planning for a new project. The time was not right, the month was not right; he had more than enough to do already. He finished his sandwich, sipped the whisky, let his mind drift pleasurably in contemplation of the work yet to be done on his living canvas.

When he glanced in the girl's direction her eyes slipped over him again and he took a deep breath. He was certain he detected a gleam of interest in her glance, a possible invitation. There would be no harm in sounding out the possibilities. The woman presently in the cellar, he had grabbed her off the street, unlike the first two, and there was something unsatisfying about that. It was better to get to know the woman who would become his project, even if only superficially; his art should reflect the reality of the subject's personality even if the design was already predetermined. And this woman, here in the bar . . . there could be no harm in finding out about her, weighing up the possibilities, contemplating in advance the excitement and the opportunity that her flesh could provide him. If the opportunity arose.

He pushed aside the empty sandwich plate, picked up his whisky and strolled across the bar to stand in front of the woman in the corner. He smiled. 'Hi. I think I've seen you here before.'

She returned his smile and shrugged. 'It's likely. I'm becoming a regular. I work close by and it's a suitable watering hole to relax in at the end of a tiring day.'

He stood in front of her, rocking slightly on his heels, holding her glance. 'The lady who left . . . she work with you?'

The woman nodded, finished her drink. 'Yeah, that's right. We slave for an accounting firm. But she's got a heavy date this evening.'

'Leaving you high and dry.' He widened his smile and gestured towards the bar. 'Can I get you a drink?'

She hesitated, stared at him, chewed her lip thoughtfully, then glanced at her empty glass and shrugged, making up a mind that he guessed was already leaning that way. 'Why not? I'll have a Campari, if that's OK.'

He nodded, turned, went back to the bar and ordered himself another whisky, draining the remains of the one in his hand while the barman fulfilled the order. When he returned to the woman's table he placed the Campari in front of her and extended his hand, introducing himself. The usual pseudonym: Peter.

'Paula,' she replied, taking his hand. 'Peter and Paula!' Her grip was surprisingly firm. He slid into the seat beside her. She moved away slightly to give him more room and looked at him appraisingly. 'And I guess this must be one of your regular haunts.'

He grimaced, and looked about him. 'More or less. But I don't live around here. I'm an artist, so I tend to move around a fair bit, looking for locations, seeking inspiration, that sort of thing.'

There was a gleam of playful provocation in her eyes as she grinned at him. 'So does picking up girls in a bar count as inspiration?'

'I don't make a practice of it, but who knows?' he laughed.

'Who knows indeed,' she replied, and there was a hint of suggestiveness in her tone.

She was easy to talk to. She was reluctant to discuss her job on the ground that it was boring and since she was at it all day she wanted to leave it behind her. They talked about music, though her range was somewhat limited, he felt; she declared she was a fan of the Terminator movies, which rather surprised him; she did not impress him with her depth of reading. But she was easy company and for a while the tensions that had been in his body were relieved, and he relaxed, had another drink or two.

Then, quite suddenly, he remembered the pharmacy. He glanced at his watch. 'Damn!'

'You in a hurry?' she asked teasingly.

'Huh . . . there's something I've got to do. I'm sorry, I have to leave, Paula.' Awkwardly, cursing inwardly, he got to his feet, finishing his drink in a quick swallow. He was cutting things fine. He blinked, enjoying the inadvertent pun. He hesitated, standing there, looking down at her. 'But if you work close by, I guess you might use this pub again.'

She shrugged indifferently. She seemed a little piqued at his sudden decision to leave. 'Wednesdays and Fridays, usually.'

'Maybe we'll meet up here again.'

She was slow to respond, as though she were a little annoyed, but finally she nodded. 'Yeah. OK. That would be nice. I've enjoyed meeting you.'

'And I you. See you then. Next Wednesday?'

She shrugged. 'I'll be here.'

He would probably return also. If he felt it was right. But no decisions yet. No commitments. No plans except those he would work out in his head. Later. He smiled at her, turned, left the bar and closed the door behind him. He glanced at his watch again. He hurried around to the pharmacy. It would be closing in ten minutes.

The purchase was quickly made, the shop assistant glancing at her watch, urging on the end of her day. The streets were quiet as he made his way back to the cellar. He began to tremble with anticipation as soon as he was back in the echoing warehouse. He worked his way carefully among the jumble of old boxes, scattered ironwork and discarded litter; he was aware of the scuttling of rats as he reached the stairs. They would have been attracted by the smell of blood, as usual, but the cellar was reasonably secure, and he doubted the animals would approach a living person. With one hand extended in front of him he descended the worn stairs, fumbled for the padlock and inserted the key. It moved easily, well oiled.

When he opened the door he heard the woman sobbing.

That was good. She had recovered consciousness. The smelling salts would not be necessary, though the contents of the bottle could come in useful later. It was necessary that the subject was aware as he worked, so she could feel the pain, react as he slid the scalpel into the warm flesh. He felt his way along the dark wall to the light switch. The light glared brightly in his eyes and he heard the woman cry out in panic and pain. He ignored her for the moment, crossed the room, took off his jacket and sweater, slipped on the stained shirt and returned to the seat facing her, checking the table for the scalpels and the inks.

Then he looked at her.

11

Her eyes were wide, dark brown with fear and terror, her mouth open with spittle draining from her lips. Her throat pulsed, sobs gurgling from her chest. He smiled, picked up the scalpel and leaned forward, staring at her breasts, swabbing away the drying blood with the damp cloth in his left hand, feeling the excitement rising in his chest, the warmth stealing through his body, as he inspected what he had already achieved. The delicacy, the evenness, the *artistry* of his carving.

'Please,' the woman begged through her strangling sobs. 'Please stop. Don't kill me . . . don't hurt me . . .'

He was hardly aware of her words. His concentration was total. The design was so clear in his mind as he leaned forward and began to add to the project, cutting deeper, tracing outlines he had already made with inks, deeper and deeper, and when she began to scream again he felt the power within him expand, frenzy gripping his lower stomach as his eyes widened. The sweat poured from him and his horizons expanded, far beyond this dark cellar, to the blue sky and hay fields and colour. . . .

And death.

CHAPTER ONE

1

Inevitably, the courtroom at Newcastle Crown Court was crowded.

There had been the expected considerable inquisitive and noisy crowd gathered at Wesley Square but not many had managed to obtain entry. The courtroom was packed and the seats allocated to the press were full: the accredited representatives seemed to have flooded in from leading nationals and local weeklies, and radio and television reporters were also present. The public seats held a wide variety of individuals, but women were notable by their presence in numbers, and there had already been some scenes during the presentation of the evidence for the prosecution, with two people being ejected after demonstrations of their anger and hatred in court, directed towards the man charged with being the Zodiac Killer.

Eric Ward leaned back in his seat, watching as Sharon Owen prepared herself to attack the witness on the stand. He had briefed her and she was responding with all the skill that he knew she possessed. He glanced across to the prosecuting counsel. Quentin Pryce, a hook-nosed, middle-aged barrister of gloomy disposition, had been drafted in from the Midlands, presumably because of his earlier knowledge of the case, and he was looking distinctly uncomfortable, as he had good reason to be. The prosecution was foundering, he was aware of it as much as was the judge.

Mr Justice Abernethy, a portly, red-faced man with a suspicious eye and a stubborn chin, was leaning back on the bench, his brow furrowed thoughtfully, his pendulous lip thrust out as he watched Sharon flip quickly through the papers in front of her before raising her head to stare intently at the witness. He was aware it was all a performance, a slow building up of tension before she spoke to the witness. He had seen it all before: he knew the tricks of counsel. But Eric was also aware Abernethy was concerned at the thinness of the prosecution case. He would know which way Sharon was heading.

She was a different person in the courtroom, Eric thought. He had known her in a professional capacity for three years now but it was only six months ago that he had finally allowed himself to respond to the clear attraction she had shown for him. They had met for lunch several times – her chambers were close to his own office on the Quayside – but their relationship had only become close after an initial weekend at a hotel in the Cheviots where nothing had been hurried, but each had taken the opportunity to get to know the other better, away from the courts and professional business. It had been a pleasurable experience, and after that first time they had seen a great deal of each other, taking opportunities to meet two or three times a week at the Quayside for lunch, weekends at the coast, an occasional visit to London when one or the other had business there. In the country they had enjoyed taking long walks; they had discovered tucked-away restaurants in small villages in the Northumberland countryside; in Newcastle they had attended concerts at The Sage, and drama productions at the Theatre Royal in Grey Street. She was an intelligent, beautiful woman, they were both single and attracted to each other, and they were enjoying their time together.

'So is it serious?' his ex-wife Anne had asked him when they happened to meet at a charity dinner in Morpeth.

'Is what serious?' he countered.

'Sharon Owen and you.' When he raised his eyebrows in mock surprise, she said, 'Oh, come on, Eric, it's hardly a mystery. You've been seen together often enough recently. And don't try telling me it's just a professional relationship!'

It was some years since he and Anne had divorced; he supposed they had each been partly to blame for the collapse of their marriage. There had been some difficult moments during the early years after the break-up but any hints of acrimony had long since passed away. They were now friends, occasionally a little edgy in the relationship, but essentially they had gone their own ways, Anne with her business interests and the management of her estates at Sedleigh Hall, Eric with his Quayside law practice. She still called upon him for his professional services from time to time, but he retained his independence in his own practice, even though she constantly told him he could do better in the commercial sector in Newcastle. But his was a practice which suited him after his years on the beat as a police officer on Tyneside and it was a practice that had grown considerably in the last two years. His secretary, Susie Cartwright, had become much busier since briefs from the Treasury, the Foreign and Commonwealth Office and the Home Office had started coming in. The increase in activity had led to his taking rooms on another floor of the building overlooking the river, and he had found it necessary to employ two junior solicitors to assist him in the general running of the business.

Their presence allowed him to concentrate on the extension of his criminal practice. It was work he was at ease with and he had been able to hand over to them most of the extra work that had come his way: it was interesting how his client list had grown once it was known he was handling government briefs. And that extension had led to a consequent greater use of the forensic skills of Sharon Owen.

'Let's just say Sharon and I enjoy each other's company,' Eric had insisted to Anne. 'And leave it there.'

She had had the good sense to do so.

The present brief, of course, had not come from the official sources that had been developing ever since his involvement with the Anubis affair: Guardian of the Dead, he thought grimly, an apposite name, given the circumstances of the case that had led to several deaths. But one of the results of that affair had been a flow of briefs for prosecutions: he had reached a certain tacit agreement with the Home Office. His discretion and silence were assured by their becoming a client of his.

This case had come out of the blue. On this occasion he was acting for the defence, and he had had no hesitation in briefing Sharon Owen to act on behalf of Raymond Conroy.

He and Sharon had discussed the matter at some length over dinner at a restaurant overlooking the Tyne. From where they sat they were able to see the gleaming outline of The Sage Centre and the Millennium Bridge. The floating nightclub located on board the *Tuxedo Princess* had now left the river, the boat having sailed to a new home in Greece, but lights still gleamed along the quayside, gaudily lit pleasure boats sliding downriver to the mouth of the Tyne.

The river had swirled blackly below them, glittering balefully in the full moon, as he and Sharon had talked.

'I have to admit, I have reservations about taking this defence brief,' Sharon had said quietly. He could detect the anxiety in her tone and see it in her eyes.

'The nature of the case, you mean. I understand. But we're officers of the court,' Eric had reminded her. 'In situations like this we ... or you at least ... have little choice but to agree to act.'

She shook her golden head. 'I know we barristers have an obligation to act for a client whether we like it or not, but I have to admit this one leaves a bad taste in my mouth. I'm not exactly looking forward to meeting this individual.' She grimaced, glancing doubtfully at Eric. 'I would have expected this case to have been heard in the Midlands. It was a surprise when it was scheduled for Newcastle.'

Eric shrugged. 'You can see the reasons for it.'

'Too much local publicity? Prejudice?' She grimaced. 'It's usually the defence who raise that as an issue and ask that the trial be moved to a court outside the immediate area.'

Eric nodded. 'That's right. Usually on the grounds that local feeling is running too high and it would be difficult to empanel a jury who would not be biased.'

'Precisely. But in this case it's the prosecution who made the request to the Lord Chancellor. It's unusual.'

Eric picked up his wine glass, stared into the twinkling red of the liquid and grimaced thoughtfully. 'Yes ... I've been thinking about it. I've got this suspicion that they're worried. Fine, they've got the CPS go ahead to agree that the prosecution could be brought but I wonder whether they really believe the case against Conroy is all that strong. It's circumstantial, of course—'

'Nothing wrong with that.'

'I agree. But I've spoken at length with Conroy, and he's raised some doubts about motives, and actions, and the evidence they're going to bring, well . . . if you agree to take the case you'll see it raises certain problems for the prosecution. I think they've acted precipitately.'

'You might be right. Anyway, you want me at least to talk to Conroy,' Sharon said soberly.

'If you're going to take the case, you'll need to see him.'

She sighed. 'As you say, I don't have much choice since I've no excuse to offer by way of pressure of work. And the seniors in my chambers are more than happy to leave it to me. In fact, I have the distinct impression most of them don't want to touch this particular piece of business. I have to admit I'm reluctant because of the details that have already emerged in the press, after the preliminary hearing. As far as I've already read in the newspapers, the facts are pretty grisly, and if this is the guy who committed these horrific murders—'

'The prosecution have yet to persuade a jury of that,' Eric reminded her.

She glanced out of the window at the dark river and nodded in resignation. 'I know. Well, better fix it up, Eric.' She shook herself and smiled at him. 'Now . . . I think we ought to concentrate on enjoying our dinner.'

Raymond Conroy.

Eric glanced at the man in the dock. Conroy had dressed as he had been advised by his lawyers, in a well-cut, sober, dark grey business suit, white shirt, neat tie. His short black hair had been recently trimmed, black curls thinning at the crown of the head. He had grey eyes, heavy lidded under arched, clearly defined eyebrows, and a soft-lipped, sensuous mouth. His features were lean, slightly hollow-cheeked, his nose thin and straight, his cheekbones prominent. Overall it was a handsome face and yet there was something *unmade* about it. Eric was left with the impression that something was missing in the man's appearance. It was difficult to be precise but perhaps it was in some strange way a lack of humanity: there was a coldness about his appearance, an arrogant detachment as though he was divorced from his surroundings, watching what was happening around him with a cool distancing, an indifference not only to what was happening in the courtroom but to life in general. He was an unmoved, uninvolved observer – or at least gave the impression of being so.

There had been the same kind of cold indifference on Conroy's part when Eric had interviewed him with Sharon Owen in the holding room at Durham Prison.

The two lawyers had sat facing the accused man for almost two minutes, saying nothing. Conroy had sat there in his standard prison uniform, arms folded over his lean chest, his breathing apparently well under control, a vagueness about his glance as he waited for Sharon Owen to speak. She had stared at him, watching him, studying him, weighing him up. He seemed unmoved. Eric felt the unease in her, aware that she was trying hard to control her tone, so that her own personal prejudices were not displayed. At last, she murmured, 'Mr Conroy.'

It was as though she had flicked a switch: he blinked, he smiled, he leaned forward. 'You can call me Raymond.' His voice was well modulated, quiet, reserved but friendly in a surreal way. 'Please do.'

'Mr Conroy,' Sharon repeated firmly, 'you are accused of the murder of three women in the Birmingham and King's Heath area: Jean Capaldi, Dorothy Chance and Irene Dixon.'

Raymond Conroy smiled lazily. 'Charges to which I pleaded not guilty when arraigned at the magistrates court.'

Conroy's eyes seemed carelessly unfocused, but his tone was deep, lacked strain, and underlined the confidence he displayed in his bearing.

'The details of these crimes are of a particularly horrifying nature,' Sharon went on coldly. 'They involve torture, mutilation and strangulation. You are aware of these details?'

Raymond Conroy twitched his nostrils in distaste and raised his head. He shrugged indifferently. 'Isn't everyone? We all read the newspapers, watch television. The gutter press have had a field day. What do they call the man who did these things? The Zodiac Killer. A cheap sensationalism. Even the more respectable newspapers have run leading articles. Oh, yes, I've read the details . . . at least those which have been stated in the media. Torture, the carving of what the newspapers have described as esoteric designs on the breasts of these unfortunate women, final strangulation.'

'No rape,' Sharon said quietly.

'As you say.' In the short silence that followed he held her gaze, his grey eyes betraying nothing. 'Not what one might call a normal sexual motive, then. If rape can be regarded as a normal activity in the human male. The curious thing is, so many women have written to me since I was arrested. Offering sympathy. And other things. Even marriage. Odd, isn't it? I wonder what motivates them to wish to form a relationship with me.' He smiled thinly. 'Rather ghoulish, don't you think? But apparently not unusual. The fact that I might be the killer, or not, seems to make little difference.'

Sharon shuffled uneasily on her chair. 'What are your personal views about these killings?'

Raymond Conroy's eyes were glazed and icy. He lifted

one shoulder in a deprecating gesture. 'Do I need to have any? I have no particular feelings about them. They don't affect me. I never made the acquaintance of any of these unfortunate women.'

'But you're charged with the murders.'

He nodded, a mock-serious frown appearing on his brow. 'Yes, I have been charged, but it's clear I've been set up – *framed* as our American cousins would say – to hide what can only be described as police incompetence. The police have to find someone, don't they? It's been over a year since the first murder was perpetrated. They've been under considerable pressure. The media have been on their backs. There have been questions asked in parliament. A chief constable has been forced to resign after one botched operation, when the man they arrested turned out to be innocent. Demands for action have been made. Public demonstrations, slogan chanting, banner waving, the kind of public hysteria one associates normally with the French. Over there, they are so addicted to their *manifestations*, aren't they? But among the sober citizens of towns in the Midlands? Perhaps it's a result of so much immigration from excitable foreigners gathering in hysterical communities. Not realizing we don't do things that way in this country. Till now, at least. However, a deal of pressure. So the police had finally to take action. But they've brought trumped-up charges against an innocent man. Me. They won't get away with it. At least,' he added with a wintry smile, 'not as long as you do your job properly.'

Sharon glanced at Eric, took a deep breath, leaned back in her chair, and said to the man facing her, 'You seem unusually relaxed about all this, given the nature of the accusations.'

Raymond Conroy raised an interrogative eyebrow as

though he considered the comment quaintly obtuse. 'I believe in the English legal system. The prosecution have to prove my guilt. And I'm an innocent man. Should I display anxiety? Should I be demonstrably unnerved?' He smiled. 'Who knows? When this is all over, I might find a wider clientele for my work. My painting, that is. Not the handiwork the prosecution is attempting to thrust upon me. Zodiac designs carved on human flesh. Art? Really!'

Eric could sense Sharon's anger at the man's cold insouciance. She was silent for a little while, then she shuffled among the papers Eric had supplied her. 'There seems to be little in the prosecution case that clearly links you with the first two killings: Dorothy Chance and Jean Capaldi. The prosecution is proceeding on the basis that there are considerable similarities in the *modus operandi* of the three murders. Their main effort will be devoted to an attempt to establish your guilt in relation to the death of the third woman.'

'So it would seem.'

Sharon stared at him curiously. 'There is some forensic evidence which would seem to implicate you in the murder of that third victim, quite clearly. DNA samples on a scalpel, for instance. The scalpel was found at your flat, I believe?'

'*A* scalpel was found there,' Conroy corrected her, with a twisted, dismissive smile.

'You're not a doctor.'

'I'm a painter,' Conroy asserted. 'I use oils. At various stages during the work on my canvases I use a scalpel to remove, or add, layers of paint. It's hardly a criminal offence, using such a tool, and of itself it can hardly support a charge of murder.'

'Even if the scalpel in question carries DNA evidence?'

'It's inevitable it would carry my DNA if I was in the habit

22

of using it regularly.'

'The evidence is of DNA from the murdered prostitute, Irene Dixon. Traces of her blood.'

'Minute, I understand.'

'Her blood, nevertheless,' Sharon persisted. 'The amount is hardly important. The fact of its existence is enough!'

'Then it's not my scalpel. Or if it is, the DNA was planted on the scalpel *after* it was taken from my flat.'

Sharon's mouth twisted; Eric was aware that she was constrained by her dislike of the cold, arrogant tones of the man she was to defend in court. She turned over a sheet of the notes Eric had provided. 'You were seen in the area where Irene Dixon's body was found.'

Raymond Conroy pinched his elegant nostrils with his index finger and thumb. He shrugged. 'A derelict quayside area frequented by drop-outs and drug addicts, cheek by jowl with a newly built office area, and some pubs not merely frequented by working men but becoming fashionable among professional people tired of drinking in modern music-tainted, run-of-the-mill brewery monstrosities. A considerable number of people attend the area in the evenings. That's hardly a crime.'

Eric knew what he was talking about. He preferred pubs with a certain amount of character himself.

'So what were you doing there?'

'Doing? My dear lady, what does one normally do in such places? Relaxing, of course. In the pubs, having a drink. Otherwise . . . there had been some publicity about the area. Derelict, about to be redeveloped. I went there for inspiration. Visual experiences. Dying industry. Deserted canal. End of an industrial era. Have you seen any of my canvases?'

Sharon held his glance and nodded. 'They're very dark.'

23

Conroy smiled cynically. 'Does that denote a criminal mind? I paint what I see. And what I feel.'

'Do you use inks?'

'No. The occasional watercolour, after preliminary sketches. Then oils. The murderer, I understand from what I've read in the papers and from what was stated in the magistrates hearing, used inks both to outline his ... designs, so-called, and then to colour certain areas thereafter. After the carving of the flesh. Interesting technique.'

There was a sudden tension in the room. 'I presume you've been shown some of these ... designs. What do you think of them?' Sharon asked.

Raymond Conroy frowned. He seemed lost in thought for a little while. His heavy-lidded eyes flickered to the window and he pursed his lips. 'Signs of the Zodiac. They display a certain ... ability, I suppose. Carved in outline, coloured in different inks, concentrated on the breast area. They have what one might describe as a kind of precision. The prosecution says they're the product of a warped imagination. And I suppose that may be so; they appear to me to have been driven by some kind of compulsion. Or maybe it's just a game, a psychologically driven attempt to reach out to some neurotic link with the stars, or antiquity, or whatever ... I'm not a psychoanalyst, of course. And I'm really only commenting upon some of the theories already put forward by the so-called psychiatric experts for the prosecution. But all artists of any calibre proceed under some kind of compulsion. However, as to the designs themselves ... I have to say, they're not quite my style.' He smiled thinly. 'Nor were they executed on the sort of canvas I prefer.'

Eric recalled the shudder he had felt run through Sharon

when he escorted her from the room. After the interview they came out of the prison, and she took a deep breath of fresh air. They left their papers in Eric's car and then walked along the street leading down the hill to the river. They strolled along the shaded banks for half an hour, saying little, before climbing up to the eleventh-century cathedral that had grown on the site of the ancient White Church of the Lindisfarne monks. They wandered through the College Green and the cloisters of the Benedictine monastery to the Norman castle given to William the Conqueror by Bishop Walcher, high on the bluff above the loop of the river. They had little to say to each other until Eric suggested they cross to the Market Place and take a coffee in Saddler Street. She sat huddled in a corner of a café, near the window, staring out at people passing by in front of them. Ordinary people. He joined her with two cups of coffee.

'So, what do you think?'

She glanced at him and shrugged. 'Does it matter? I'm committed to defending him. And there's no doubt we can attack the forensic evidence, from what he's told us. If it's true. But he's a cold bastard.'

'Even cold bastards deserve a good defence submission.'

She sighed, and nodded. 'That's right. And from the points raised in your brief, I think we'll have something to work on.'

And now she was just about to do that.

2

'Detective Constable Paula Gray.'

'That is correct.'

Her dark hair was brushed back neatly, close to her head.

Her brown eyes were serious and intense as they held Sharon Owen's gaze. There was a certain determination in her features, but her mouth was wide and generous, and she held her head up proudly as though aware of the importance of her situation, anxious to present herself as well as possible, and withstand with commitment the cross-examination Sharon was about to commence.

'How long have you been a detective, Miss Gray?' Sharon asked.

Paula Gray squared her shoulders. 'Three weeks.'

'So you've been assigned to the plain clothes division only recently, since your work on this case.'

'That is correct.'

Sharon inclined her head slightly, and nodded. 'So congratulations are due. This will have been an ambition of yours, to get out of uniform?'

Paula Gray shrugged. 'I suppose so.'

'And no doubt you will now be looking forward to extend your career in the force, obtain promotion, move on to better things.'

Stiffly, Paula Gray replied, 'We all hope for promotion in due course, when it is worked for and deserved.'

Sharon smiled at her. 'Quite so. But you were still in uniform during the progress of this case. We have heard from senior officers involved in this investigation and I fear I remain somewhat puzzled by the part you seem to have played in it. As I understand your own evidence, you were a junior member of a team of some thirty officers investigating the so-called Zodiac murders.'

'That is correct.'

Sharon nodded, stood erect, folded her arms as she held the gaze of the woman in the witness box. 'Just exactly what was your role in the group?'

DC Gray shrugged. 'I was just one of the team. I undertook such tasks as I was allocated from time to time. A lot of it was routine. House-to-house enquiries, collating information, checking data, interviewing particular leads.'

'I suppose you received a great deal of help from the public?'

'There was a considerable interest in the killings. Many local people came forward with information, suggestions, possible leads. It all had to be pulled together, checked out, information sifted . . .'

'And I suppose there was a fair number of suspects?'

DC Gray scratched her cheek and grimaced. 'There were people in the files we had to check out. We used HOLMES, of course, the central computerized system for possible suspects. No obvious leads. A few with known form. But we were able to eliminate them. In fact, we'd sort of come to a dead end at one point.' She stopped, as though unwilling to go further with the thought and embarrassingly aware of the unconscious pun.

'So at what point of time did the investigation concentrate on the accused?'

Paula Gray's eyes flickered briefly towards the sharply suited, indifferent figure of Raymond Conroy. His eyes held hers and a faint smile touched his lips. She looked away and in a tightly controlled tone she replied, 'It was relatively late in the investigation.'

'And what was it that caused suspicion to fall upon the accused?'

DC Gray took a deep breath. 'We had followed several lines of enquiry but finally we felt that we were able to isolate a particular area around the Midland Canal where it was likely the killer was operating.'

'From the location of the three bodies.'

'Among other pointers. As has already been explained, we enlisted the aid of forensic pathologists and forensic psychiatrists. From their suggestions we were able to build up a picture, a profile of the person likely to be responsible for the killings. Age, ethnicity, educational standard, marital status, professional ability, that sort of thing. And we were also able to identify the likely residential and operational areas of the killer. These were only pointers, of course, but it helped us concentrate, focus our attentions, so to speak.'

'So am I right in suggesting that you finally fixed on Raymond Conroy because he appeared in the area regularly, even though he did not live there, and was known to be a single man with artistic leanings?'

DC Gray hesitated. 'They were matters that we found of interest. We received background information from a number of people who knew him by sight, had seen him around. There was a feeling that he sort of stood out, if you know what I mean. Didn't quite fit in, that sort of thing. An outsider. But on the other hand, he fitted the profile that we had been given.'

'Forensic profile. Geographical locations.' Sharon consulted her notes, and changed the direction of her questions. 'Interesting. . . . Now it is clear from the forensic evidence obtained from the victims that the women in question were not murdered in the locations in which they were found. The first woman, Dorothy Chance, was discovered half-hidden in a ditch close to a country park not far from the canal; the second, Jean Capaldi, in a stream near a disused viaduct. The final corpse was found near a salvage scrapyard, dumped perhaps hurriedly, with no attempt to hide the body.'

Paula Gray pursed her lips. 'We think the killer had been disturbed while he was getting rid of his victim. She was probably destined for the canal.'

'Though you've turned up no witnesses to the dumping of the bodies. And am I right in saying that in spite of the extensive investigations you carried out in the area you never succeeded in identifying the actual location where the murders had been committed?'

'As I've explained, the bodies were found in various locations around and near the Midland Canal,' Paula Gray confirmed, 'but no, we never managed to locate the actual place where the murders were committed.' She hesitated briefly. 'There can be little doubt that the atrocities were carried out over a period of time in a location which would have been isolated, under the control of the accused, not overlooked. No one seems to have seen the initial abductions; no screams have been reported, so we assume that the crimes were carried out in some secure location. The women would seem to have been kept by the killer for several days. He had a safe house. Still as yet unknown to us.'

'Of course,' Sharon murmured almost casually, 'if you *had* found this location, a dungeon, a cellar, a room in a house or apartment under the control of the accused, it would have been of considerable assistance to your investigation. I mean, you would have almost inevitably discovered traces of blood, clothing, artefacts such as the ropes or chains used to restrain the victims, along with, possibly, a considerable array of DNA samples on which your forensic team could have worked. Evidence which would have clearly linked the accused to the crimes.'

'That is correct.'

'But you have not, up to this time, ever found the hidden location . . .' Sharon nodded thoughtfully. 'In fact, am I right in stating that there is no forensic evidence to connect the accused to the murders of the first two women, and the only piece of evidence, as far as DNA is concerned, which connects Raymond Conroy to the third victim, Irene Dixon, amounts to traces of dried blood on a scalpel, possibly used to carve designs on the breasts of the dead woman?'

'That is so,' the detective constable agreed, a certain reluctance staining her tone.

Sharon shuffled the papers in front of her, and glanced across to the dock. Raymond Conroy smiled at her, nodding slightly. Sharon's eyes returned to the woman in the witness box. 'So let me get this clear. Your team came to the conclusion that they would be likely to find the killer operating in a deserted factory and dilapidated quayside area near the Midland Canal, and that the person in question would have artistic leanings. On the basis of the careful, *artistic* Zodiac designs carved on these unfortunate women?'

Paula Gray's features stiffened at the mockery in Sharon's tone. 'We dealt with what we had. Forensic reports, psychiatric reports, surveys of the location of the killings, the careful tracing of the carvings all played their part. The combination led us to the accused. And finally, to positive DNA evidence.'

Sharon nodded. 'Ah, yes. The scalpel . . .' She paused, eyeing the witness curiously. 'Where was the scalpel found?'

'In the flat belonging to and used by Raymond Conroy.'

'Who actually found it?'

'It was located by Detective Sergeant Arlington.'

'In the course of a search of the premises owned by the accused.'

'That is correct,' DC Gray stated firmly.

In an almost offhand tone, Sharon Owen asked, 'The search was legal, of course, backed by a search warrant?'

'Of course.'

Sharon brushed away an errant lock of blonde hair from her eyes; her fingers wandered down her cheek to rest, touching her lips thoughtfully as she held the glance of the woman in the witness box. 'DC Arlington found the scalpel. Who was it first made contact with Raymond Conroy, in the course of the investigation?'

'Who first questioned him, you mean?'

'That's not what I asked,' Sharon corrected her. 'Who made the first *contact*?'

There was a short silence. 'That would have been me,' Paula Gray admitted carefully.

'How did that come about?'

'We met sort of casually, in a pub.'

'Casually? By chance? Or were you acting under instructions at that time?'

The witness hesitated, then nodded. 'I was acting under orders. That is correct.'

Eric leaned forward in the silence that followed. Sharon Owen had proceeded with care to this point, but now she was about to make use of the claims that her client in the dock had made. In the long discussions that had taken place in Durham Prison, neither Eric nor Sharon could be certain that Raymond Conroy had told them the truth but it was about to be tested in the courtroom.

'Can you explain the circumstances of the first meeting?'

Paula Gray's tongue flickered over her lips. She took a deep breath. 'We had been making enquiries in the area for some time and we received various information about the habits of the accused, his use of certain pubs in the area. I was instructed to attend one of these pubs.'

'To seek out Raymond Conroy?'

'Yes.'

'Why him?'

31

Paula Gray's tone was careful. 'His name had come up. Or at least, his description. He didn't talk to many people. And he was thought a bit . . . odd. An outsider in the area.'

'When you met him, you were in uniform?'

'Of course not.'

'Of course not. How were you dressed?'

The witness frowned, shrugged. 'I can't remember exactly.'

Sharon smiled. 'But I imagine it would have been casually. An attractive woman, dressed for an evening in a local pub. So the idea was to try to attract his attention, perhaps get into conversation with him.'

DC Gray hesitated. 'That is correct.'

'And did he make contact?'

'Almost immediately. Yes. When he saw I was alone, he approached me. We had a drink together. After that, there were other occasions, several conversations.'

Sharon raised her eyebrows. 'Other occasions? Several conversations? Was a record kept of these meetings? Were you wired, for instance?'

After a moment's hesitation, the detective constable nodded. 'I was wearing a wire, yes. For my own safety as much as anything else. There was a back-up team in the area. We could not be certain what would happen.'

Sharon nodded, frowning. 'But no record of these . . . conversations have been put forward in evidence.'

Paula Gray shrugged. 'There was nothing on the tapes which could help us.'

'The conversations between the two of you were *innocent*, you mean?'

Paula Gray wriggled slightly. 'You could say that. But I still felt uncomfortable. There was something about him, his attitude. . . .'

'So the continued meetings . . . they were effected because you felt *uncomfortable* about him. Yet there was nothing said, specifically, which could have connected him to the killings?'

DC Gray chewed at her lip. 'Well, not really. Nothing that could be produced for evidentiary purposes. But we did talk about the murders. He didn't seem to take them seriously.'

'How do you mean?'

'He seemed to think the women had been prostitutes and were facing the kind of risks that . . . but in fact only one of the women had been working the streets. I didn't like his attitude. I reported it. We were suspicious of him. I discussed it with the team and it was then decided we should seek a warrant to search his premises.'

'For the scalpel.'

Paula Gray's eyes were suddenly watchful. 'Not specifically, no. Of course not. We had no idea what we might find. As it happened—'

Sharon held up an imperious hand, stopping her from continuing. 'One moment. I'm puzzled. Without having any specific reasons for suspecting the accused in the first instance, other than that he was an artist who frequented the area, visited pubs, talked to local women, and was thought by locals to be a bit *odd*, you were instructed to deliberately make an attempt to speak with him, make his acquaintance . . . but then found that his conversations were upsetting, but essentially innocent.'

'I didn't say—'

'The tapes of your conversations weren't considered useful to the investigation! So one can only presume they would have been nothing more than friendly, innocent banter, perhaps – a man chatting up an attractive woman! Yet on the basis that he failed to think or talk seriously about the murders in the area, a search warrant was obtained to turn over his flat, find something that might link him to the murder of these women?'

'There were other pointers! He stood out in the area, he was always hanging around there, and he fitted the forensic profile information we had! Single, artistic, a loner. We felt there was something *odd* about Conroy, a coldness, a sort of indifference, something that made us believe he might be the man we were looking for!'

'So a search warrant was obtained, on such flimsy suspicions?' Sharon shook her head in mock despair. 'But now tell me, exactly *when* was the search warrant sought?'

'I'm not sure what you—'

'When was the warrant applied for, in relation to your meetings with the accused? To be more precise, how long after you had *personally* visited Conroy's apartment, Detective Constable Gray?'

There was a brief silence. Paula Gray's eyes widened. 'I don't know what you mean!'

'Surely you know *exactly* what I mean! What was the lapse of time between your first visit to Conroy's apartment and the issue of the search warrant?' Sharon paused, then leaned forward, speaking carefully and clearly. 'Let me put to you exactly what occurred. Under instructions from your senior officers you, a junior member of the team but perhaps the most attractive one, made the acquaintance of Raymond Conroy casually, in a pub. You met a second time, and struck up a closer friendship. When he later suggested that you go to his flat with him, you agreed. He's a handsome, unattached man; you're a good-looking, single woman. This was nothing more than a honey trap!'

'It was nothing of the sort!'

'He did not know you were a police officer. He was

attracted to you. He invited you to his flat. And you agreed, because you had been instructed to find out as much about him as you possibly could. And if you could find out what was wanted, it would mean a success for you, a movement to the detective squad, maybe later promotion, a feather in your cap. And when he made the perhaps inevitable approaches to you, at the apartment, in the call of duty,' Sharon asserted scornfully, 'you did not resist.'

'This is rubbish!' the witness expostulated, but there was fear in her eyes.

'I put it to you, Detective Constable Gray, that in your eagerness to find out more about this man, you got carried away, you succumbed to his advances, you slept with him, not once but several times, and in the course of using his apartment you had occasion to see where and how he worked. You saw that he used a scalpel when working in oils, and when you reported this fact back to your superior officers the decision was made to take out a search warrant. Perhaps, as you suggest, it was to find incriminating evidence in general terms, but also, specifically, to lay hands on the scalpel you'd seen among his effects.'

'This isn't true,' Paula Gray asserted vehemently.

'What isn't true? That you didn't see the scalpel when you were there?'

'I didn't—'

'You're not going to deny you and Raymond Conroy were lovers, are you?'

'We never—'

'You're not about to claim you never went to the apartment with him? Or deny that you saw the scalpel there? Or perhaps take the opportunity to *plant* the scalpel in the apartment, the one that you had found beside the body of the third victim? Or perhaps one you tainted with DNA evidence, to bring a case against an innocent man?'

Counsel for the prosecution was on his feet, protesting. 'While a certain latitude is allowed in cross-examination of a witness, I must protest here that in this instance the witness is not even being allowed to provide answers to the ridiculous charges counsel for the defence is making!' Quentin Pryce rubbed his prominent nose, glaring at Sharon. 'Badgering the witness is hardly a suitable way of carrying on a cross-examination.'

There was a tense silence in the courtroom. There had been no response to prosecuting counsel from the bench: it was almost as though Mr Justice Abernethy had not heard prosecuting counsel. His eyes were fixed on the witness, and his brow was thunderous. Sharon stared at Detective Constable Gray. 'Are you prepared to answer the questions I have asked? How many times did you visit Raymond Conroy's apartment?'

The witness seemed petrified, a rabbit caught in the headlights.

'Were you and Conroy lovers?' Sharon continued more quietly. 'Did you allow him to seduce you in order to obtain his trust? Did you then abuse that trust by placing a stained scalpel in the apartment?'

'You can't say I would do something like that,' Paula Gray gasped.

'You were all under pressure in your team,' Sharon asserted. 'I put it to you that you were encouraged to get close to the accused, and help the investigation a little further down the line. You went along with that, but when it didn't seem to be getting anywhere nearer the solution you were seeking, your senior officers suggested to you that you "find" the evidence linking Conroy to the crimes. Yes, I'm sure it was someone else who put his hand on the scalpel during the search, but it was you who told him where to look!'

Detective Constable Gray found her voice. 'That's not true! Conroy and I were never lovers! We never went to bed together when I went to his flat! I got the feeling he was . . . asexual, even. I don't think he's interested in women, not in that way! He. . . .' Her voice died away suddenly, as if she was unsure as to what she had admitted to, involuntarily. Her glance flickered around the room, resting on some of her colleagues seated in court. She seemed to want to say something more, but her voice died in her throat as uncertainty strangled her. She was put out of her misery by the judge.

Mr Justice Abernethy leaned forward on the bench. His brow was heavily lined; he glared at the witness, then at the prosecuting counsel. His pendulous lower lip was almost trembling with contempt. He turned back to the woman in the witness box. 'Let us be certain of one thing at least. Did you visit the apartment owned by the accused?'

'Yes, my lord, during the search I. . . .'

'Did you visit the apartment before the search warrant was executed?' the judge demanded in a threatening tone.

'I . . . I did not. . . .'

It was clear from his attitude that Mr Justice Abernethy did not believe her. He glared at counsel for the defence and prosecution. 'I would like to see you, in my chambers, immediately.'

The court rose as he swept indignantly from the room. Ten minutes later all three came back into the courtroom. It took only a few more minutes for Mr Justice Abernethy to thank the jury for their attendance and discharge them from any further duties. He then turned his ire on the prosecution. It was clear to him that the female officer had been instructed to begin a relationship with the accused; that she had visited his flat; and there was consequently the distinct opportunity for forensic evidence to have been created. It did not matter whether such malfeasance had in fact occurred; it was enough that there was the possibility that the police might have done so, that the opportunity was present. There had been a clear honey trap, and the forensic evidence offered in court was unsafe to rely on.

He was dismissing the prosecution; Raymond Conroy, on the evidence produced so far, was adjudged to have no case to answer.

3

After a stunned silence, the noise in the courtroom crashed about their ears.

As Raymond Conroy stepped smugly down from the dock, a surge of men and women surrounded him. Mr Justice Abernethy left the courtroom hurriedly, and court officials attempted to hold back the flood of journalists who were almost fighting to get close to Conroy. There was some shouting at the back of the court and from the corner of his eye Eric caught sight of a broad-shouldered, middle-aged man with a shock of red hair waving his fist towards Conroy and shouting, while a woman, presumably his wife, pulled at him, trying to persuade him to leave the courtroom. Her features were tear-stained, her demeanour shaken.

Sharon was already on her way to the robing room; Eric was still gathering up his papers when someone near to his elbow spoke to him. 'I guess you can understand that guy's fury.'

Eric turned his head to the speaker. The man was perhaps

in his early forties, with deep-set eyes, lean features, a thin-lipped, cynical mouth. He was of middle height, wore an old leather jacket and jeans and the collar of his shirt was frayed. He held a notebook in his left hand, and Eric gained the impression that he might be one of the more restrained members of the media pack that was attempting to obtain an interview with Raymond Conroy.

'I'm sorry ... what were you saying?' Eric asked distractedly.

'The couple at the back of the room. The guy who's shouting. It's obvious he thinks there's been a miscarriage of justice. And if you look at his face, he's enraged, wouldn't you say?'

Eric looked again at the couple near the exit of the courtroom. The woman was still pleading, dragging at the man's arm, but his face was still suffused, his eyes wild, and his fist was raised in fury. He was shouting something but Eric was unable to pick out the words in the general hubbub.

'They're the parents of one of the murdered women. His name's Jack Capaldi. Runs a chain of small pizza places in the Midlands, I believe. It looks as though he was expecting a guilty verdict – probably convinced the police had got the right man – and is furious that Conroy seems to have got away with it. Is that your view, by the way?'

It was not a question Eric was prepared to answer. 'So the Capaldis will have come up from the Midlands to attend the trial?'

'Seems so.' The speaker hesitated, then held out a hand. 'My name's Fraser, by the way. Tony Fraser.'

Eric hesitated, then shook the man's hand. 'You from the Midlands yourself?'

'Not recently. But I've been following the case, and I recognized the Capaldis from photographs published earlier in the hearings. They'd made a television appeal at one point: you know, usual thing, we must bring this monster to justice. Interesting, in view of his own background. . . . There's been a great fuss about this whole business in the Birmingham area. There was a near riot, you know, when Conroy was first arrested. A lot of people jumped to the conclusion that he was the Zodiac Killer simply because the police had made an arrest.'

Eric shrugged. 'It was why the trial was moved up here.' He hesitated, uncertain why Fraser had engaged him in conversation. 'Anyway, I'm sorry, Mr Fraser, you'll have to excuse me but I'm rather busy at the moment.'

'That's all right,' Fraser replied with a flicker of a smile. He nodded in the direction of the milling journalists. 'So are they, it seems. And they're frustrated too, now Conroy's being whisked away. Anyway, I'd like a word with you, Mr Ward, at your convenience.'

'The best thing would be to make an appointment with my secretary,' Eric replied hurriedly. Conroy was out of the dock, hustled along by police officers eager to remove the source of the bustling confusion. Sharon had vanished but Eric knew he would find her in the holding room outside the court. He nodded to Fraser, who stepped aside politely, and pushed his way past the throng, entered the robing room and then made his way along the corridor, guessing where Raymond Conroy would be taken.

Sharon Owen was already there in a private room barred to the public. When Eric entered the room Raymond Conroy was seated, staring out of the window at the Quayside, seemingly at ease, though Eric noted the pulse beating excitedly in his temple. Conroy turned his head as Eric entered, and Sharon broke away from the conversation she had been carrying on with the two police officers in plain clothes who had ushered Conroy from the courtroom and the baying pack of journalists. When Conroy saw Eric he gave a thin smile and raised a hand in welcome. He turned his head, addressing the police officers in a confident tone.

'There, gentlemen, I can assure you all will now be well, since my indefatigable solicitor has arrived. With all due deference to you, of course, Miss Owen.'

'What's happening?' Eric asked as he closed the door behind him.

Raymond Conroy waved a casual, dismissive hand. 'These two gentlemen suggest it might be as well if they stayed close, to escort me from the premises. It seems there is a back entrance and a police car waiting to whisk me away from any unpleasantness that might be occurring outside on the Quayside and around Wesley Square.'

One of the policemen glanced at Eric. He seemed irritated by Conroy's attitude, angry at the man's calmness, perhaps affected by the result of the hearing. He would not be alone, Eric considered. One of the policemen muttered bitterly, 'There's a demonstration expected outside. We don't want any trouble. It would be best if Mr Conroy came with us.'

Raymond Conroy smiled coolly. 'And I've been explaining that since I've been in the gentle custody of the upholders of the law for so many months now, I have no desire to continue to impinge upon their hospitality longer. Now that it is no longer forced upon me.'

'I'm inclined to agree with these officers,' Eric replied, a little nettled at Conroy's insouciance. 'You're clear to leave, but in the circumstances, the crowd outside, the anger at the way the case against you has collapsed. . . .'

'Due to your efforts,' Conroy acknowledged gravely.

'. . . you'd be better off getting away in their protective custody.'

Conroy raised his chin and twisted a supercilious lip. 'I disagree. I've no desire to continue my association with these gentlemen. You are still my lawyer. We have matters to settle, the question of fees due and so on, you and Miss Owen. . . .' His glance slipped towards the silent Sharon, standing just inside the doorway. 'I think it would be appropriate, and quite safe, if I were to leave the premises in *your* care, Mr Ward.'

Eric was not keen on the suggestion. He glanced at the police officers. They met his eyes; one of them shrugged indifferently. He guessed they would not press the argument if he agreed to take responsibility for the safe conduct of their former prisoner. Raymond Conroy was now a free agent. They had no jurisdiction over him. Eric bit his lip. 'I had arranged to escort Miss Owen from the building.'

'Then we can make a cosy little threesome,' Conroy suggested blandly.

Eric glanced at the barrister. Sharon's features were stiff with dislike, but her eyes were resigned. Eric sighed. 'All right. But where are you going to go?'

'I'm sure you can arrange a temporary haven for me, Mr Ward,' Conroy suggested coolly.

Eric glowered at him. He was tempted to refuse, but then thought better of it. He wanted to wash his hands of any involvement with the man. 'All right. Give me a few minutes. I'll make a couple of phone calls.'

He stepped outside, called his office, explained the situation. Susie made a couple of suggestions about accommodation. When Eric placed the second call on his mobile phone the two policemen came out of the holding room, nodded to him and made their way out to the corridor. They had given up the responsibility. When he concluded the call, Eric returned to the room where Sharon and Conroy waited for him. The room was silent; there had clearly been no conversation between them. She was staring out of the window. Conroy had an amused smirk on his lips as he contemplated her stiff back.

'All right, I think it would be as well if we waited for a while before leaving,' Eric said. 'Let's give the police time to disperse the crowds. Then I'll take you to your hotel, Mr Conroy. I've booked you a room in a quiet place in Gosforth. I don't know what your future plans might be, but I would suggest you lie low for a few days. We can conclude our business and then you can resume your life. Wherever you will.'

Conroy nodded cheerfully. 'That's fine. As for your fees . . . would you like to take a couple of my paintings in payment?'

When he saw the resentment in Eric's eyes he lifted a contemptuous eyebrow. 'Just joking, Mr Ward. Just joking.'

Two hours later, after Conroy had been delivered to his hotel under an assumed name and Eric had made the necessary arrangements about the bill, Eric suggested that Sharon came back to his apartment to relax after the tension of the trial and the subsequent hubbub in the streets. Early editions of the evening newspaper already had news of the collapse of the trial in their late bulletins: Eric guessed the morning newspapers would carry banner headlines, reflecting upon the prosecution's clumsiness and the possible repercussions now that it seemed the Zodiac Killer – whoever he might be – was still at large.

'They'll need to be careful what they write,' Eric remarked as he handed a brandy and soda to Sharon. She took the glass, cradled it in both hands and settled in her easy chair with a sigh. Eric liked the way she seemed to fit into the surroundings. He had lived alone here in the apartment for too long. But it was still early days.

'I've no doubt Abernethy's behaviour will come in for criticism,' he said, 'justified though it was. But if the newspapers imply that Conroy is the Zodiac Killer let free on the streets to kill again, our client could well bring an action for defamation, and earn quite a lot of money.'

'Just as long as he doesn't brief you and me to act on his behalf,' Sharon replied.

'You've had enough dealings with the man.'

'More than enough. He gives me the shudders,' Sharon admitted. 'And you know, I have to admit that I'm left uneasy about this whole business. I know we're not supposed to have a view about the guilt or otherwise of our clients, just to act on their behalf, do the best we can for them . . . but Raymond Conroy, well, he leaves a nasty taste in my mouth.'

Eric sat down, sipped at his own brandy. 'You think he might be the guilty man.'

Sharon shrugged. 'I think about the murdered women. And if we have helped Conroy escape, when he is the maniac responsible. . . .'

'We've just done our job,' Eric assured her. 'The evidence against him had a thin crust, circumstantial, open to abuse . . . we just drew attention to the weakness of the prosecution case. Not least that business about him and Paula Gray. How the prosecution hoped to keep the lid on that relationship, I'll never know.'

'She denied they had an affair,' Sharon reminded him.

'But she didn't deny going to his flat. I think Abernethy had no choice other than to throw the case out of court. Anyway, it's finished as far as we're concerned.'

'We have no other responsibility in the matter, you mean,'

Sharon murmured uncertainly. 'Even though we might have been instrumental in putting a killer back on the streets.'

Eric grimaced. 'Precisely. Anyway, let's not dwell on it. The business is over and done with for us.'

'It's not quite the same for some other people,' she commented wryly. 'That couple at the back of the room, for instance.'

'The red-haired guy doing the shouting. Yes, I gather he was the father of one of the murdered women, Jean Capaldi. But it's time for us all to move on.' He glanced at his watch. 'And we'll start by going out to dinner tonight.'

Sharon put her head back on the chair, and her eyes held a mischievous glint as she looked at him. 'This some way of looking for a discount from the fee I'm charging?'

Eric laughed. 'No, just seeking an opportunity for you to wear the dress that's hanging in the closet in my bedroom.'

'There's only the one. Doesn't give me much choice to create a stir in the town.'

'Maybe you ought to bring more of your clothes to the apartment. To cover eventualities.'

She smiled. 'Maybe it's not just my clothes that should move in.'

'Permanently?'

'I wouldn't want to rush matters,' she asserted, 'but the way things have been going between us, maybe we could sort of start trialing the relationship a bit more intensely. I mean, one has to be careful. I might find your personal habits too gross to handle on a regular basis.'

'I have been on my best behaviour while I'm with you,' Eric admitted with a smile.

'And if we're to shack up seriously, you need to be sure that I come from the right stock. After all, you know nothing about my background. It might be more unsavoury than you imagine.' She paused, the mocking tone fading and a slight frown appearing on her brow. 'Talking of which, there's something we should discuss. I need a lawyer.'

'You are one.'

'Tell me about it! But like they say, a lawyer who acts for himself has a fool for a client. I'll tell you about it over dinner. First, I need to finish this drink, and take a shower. I feel as though a certain grubbiness has rubbed off on me. Raymond Conroy – not one of the more savoury of my clients, and that's saying something. I'm glad we've more or less seen the last of that creepy, cold-hearted bastard.'

They left the apartment at eight in the evening. Eric had thought about driving into Newcastle to visit one of their favourite restaurants but finally was persuaded by Sharon that it would be more sensible to use one of the brasseries that had sprung up in the High Street in Gosforth. It had changed radically over recent years, with new restaurants and pavement cafés appearing to cater for university students: a café society, in spite of the northern climate. It never seemed to affect the youngsters, Eric considered: mid-thigh skirts and low-cut tops, in spite of the whistling winds of the north. Kidney trouble in the future.

They found a restaurant which advertised the excellence of its Mediterranean cuisine and they both settled for John Dory, agreeing also on the starters: scallops. Eric ordered a bottle of Pinot Grigio and they settled down in the surprisingly large room, decorated with scenes of Spanish and Portuguese villages and lifestyle.

'Somewhat forced,' Sharon murmured.

'A Gosforth view of exotic climes,' Eric suggested. 'Anyway, what's this about needing a lawyer?'

Sharon smiled and sipped her wine. 'It's a bit of a long-running affair. As is often the case with family quarrels. But that's one of the reasons I don't want to get too closely involved myself: having to dig into distant family feuds and learning a little too much about family peccadilloes makes my flesh creep. I'd rather get it all cleared up by someone other than myself. That's where you come in.'

Eric grimaced. 'Family matters can get messy.'

'Exactly. But I'd be grateful if you could look into the matter for me. There can't be much more to do. Just a matter of bringing an end to a long-running saga.'

'So what's it all about?' Eric asked.

She smiled, teasingly. 'First of all, I think you need to know that you're in danger of tying yourself in with a fairly wealthy young woman.'

'It was always your money I was after,' Eric assured her solemnly.

She grinned. 'Well, you made a good choice. The fact is, our family is pretty well loaded. Has been for a couple of generations. And that's where the problems come in.'

'Inheritance?'

'Well, yes, I suppose so. I mean, my parents – who as you know are both dead now – they left me well enough heeled through general inheritance, but there's also the matter of a trust fund which was originally set up by my grandfather. It was always separate from the money my parents left me. The trust's given rise to certain problems among the two beneficiaries. Me and my cousin. I don't want to go into details over dinner now, but if I gave you the name of the lawyer who's been handling the estate – slowly, I might add – maybe you'd be able to look into it for me, and bring the whole messy business to an end.'

Eric shrugged. 'It hardly needs saying that I'll be happy to do what I can to help.'

'There'll be a fat fee, of course,' she teased.

'I'll take it in kind.'

'I won't be averse to that.'

The remainder of the evening passed pleasantly. Eric regaled her with some of the more colourful stories about his life before he had become a lawyer, when he had been a police officer on the Tyneside beat, and she asked him about his problems with glaucoma, which he now kept under control with drugs. It was almost eleven before they left the restaurant for the short walk back to the apartment.

There was a police car some hundred yards away, its blue light flashing. It was not an unusual occurrence: with so many bars and cafés in the area there was bound to be a certain amount of drunken behaviour late at night. Sharon glanced back over her shoulder. 'Trouble?' she queried.

Eric shrugged. 'Nothing to bother lawyers, yet. The police can deal with it.' He turned his head, realized the car was stationed not very far from the hotel where he had arranged a room for Raymond Conroy and wondered briefly whether their erstwhile client had already got himself into difficulties. He shook the thought aside. He gripped Sharon's elbow firmly, steering her across the road towards his apartment.

'Come on,' he said with a smile. 'Let's go talk about lawyer's fees.'

CHAPTER TWO

1

When Eric arrived at his office on the Quayside next morning his secretary Susie Cartwright was waiting for him with his appointments book in her hand. He waved her into his room and gestured her to a seat. She sat down, tugging at the hem of her skirt in a manner that suggested she was not at ease, not best pleased with him. 'So you got that Conroy man off the charges,' she said as she raised her chin to stare challengingly at him. There was more than a hint of disapproval in her tone.

Eric eyed her carefully. Susie had been with him for a number of years now, ever since he had set up his practice on the Quayside. A widow, she was in her forties, far too young to be his mother, but that did not prevent her trying to develop such a function in their relationship: she was determined to look after him, was not afraid of telling him how he ought to go for a better kind of client, not reluctant to question some of his decisions. Occasionally she acted as his conscience, even when his conscience was not bothering him. And she had never approved of his divorce from Anne.

'We didn't exactly get him off,' he corrected her now. 'The

prosecution failed to make a case. We simply emphasized that point. Mr Justice Abernethy threw it out.'

Susie sniffed as though she was only half convinced. 'Whatever. But I have to say I didn't like the look of that man.'

'Abernethy?' Eric teased.

'Raymond Conroy,' she snapped, but he noted the reluctant ghost of a smile.

'Neither did I, particularly,' Eric admitted candidly, 'but that's not the point.'

'I'm sorry you even agreed to take the case, Mr Ward. Just when you're getting a better kind of client base as well,' she murmured with a sigh. 'Talking of which, the Home Office has been on the phone again. Mr Linwood Forster. There are three more briefs on the way. Immigration cases. And I've booked in a few new appointments for you.'

Eric accepted the appointments book she passed him. He nodded, marked two names on the list and handed the book back to her. 'I can see these people later this morning, but perhaps you'll have a word with Mr Thurston and Mr Carpenter about these others. See if they can deal with my afternoon appointments.'

Susie pursed her lips. Thurston and Carpenter, the new solicitors who had joined the practice, were young, inexperienced men straight from law school: she felt they needed protecting even more than Eric. She sniffed. 'They're pretty busy themselves, you know, and we haven't seen much of you in the office this last week.'

'That's the penalty of success, Susie,' said Eric smiling. 'Anyway, will you have a word with my two assistants? I mean, that's why I employed them: to take some of the burden from my shoulders.'

'They won't be happy, Mr Ward.' Susie hesitated and gave

the appearance of considering the matter. 'But I'll see if I can spread the work to them. Will you be out all afternoon, then?'

Eric nodded. 'I'll work on these files this morning, see these two clients, and then I'll have to be off by two. I have to go to Alnwick. I've made an appointment with the solicitors Strudmore and Evans. It's a meeting I have to attend on behalf of Miss Owen.'

Susie's lips expressed a slight disapproval. It was not that she disliked Sharon Owen: in fact she held her in considerable regard. But she had made it clear she had certain reservations about the developing relationship between her employer and the young barrister. It all went back to Anne, of course. She had always got on well with Eric's ex-wife. Her glance dropped to the appointments book. She made no further comment now, but there were silent ways in which she could express her disapproval. She stood up, stiffened her back and began to make her way back to her own room. At the door she paused, looking back at him. 'By the way, did you hear the news about Mr Conroy?'

'What about him?' Eric asked vaguely, opening one of the files in front of him.

'He was attacked last night.'

'Attacked?' Eric looked up at her and frowned. 'I arranged for him to stay at the hotel in Gosforth, the one you suggested to me, and booked him in under an assumed name. So what happened?'

Susie shook her head. 'Can't say. Just heard the gossip, that's all. Apparently he got beaten up as he came out of his hotel. The police were called immediately – there was a patrol car happened to be in the area – and they sorted it out quickly enough, it seems.'

Eric took a deep breath. He recalled the police car in the High Street near the hotel the previous evening. It was just as well he and Sharon had stayed well away from the disturbance. He was finished with Raymond Conroy. He was not surprised the man had been attacked but he wondered how he had been traced. Perhaps another guest in the hotel had recognized him. His photograph had been splashed all over the newspapers, after all. Eric had advised him to lay low, but Conroy had clearly been foolish enough to venture out from the safety of his hotel room only hours after the case against him had been dismissed. He should have had more sense, but Eric knew how arrogant the man was.

'One other thing,' Susie added. 'I had a call from a man called Fraser. Wanted to fix an appointment to see you. Today, if possible. I didn't put him in the book. I put him off in view of the other pressures on your time.' Eric wasn't absolutely certain he didn't detect a hint of irony in her tone. 'Anyway, Mr Fraser seemed reluctant to tell me what it was about. Do you know him? He said he'd already spoken to you about an appointment.'

Eric recalled the brief conversation with the somewhat shabby individual in the courtroom at the end of the trial. He thought about it for a moment, then he shrugged. 'I don't know what he wants, but ... well, if he calls again, fix something up for him. Maybe one of the others in the practice can see him.'

'Your overworked young colleagues? He specifically wants to talk to you, Mr Ward. He made that quite clear to me.'

Eric shrugged. 'So be it. But obviously not today. If you can find a time to fit him in, tomorrow or the next day, I'll see him. Now, I'll get on with these files, and I'd be grateful if I wasn't disturbed.'

'Until coffee time, I take it,' she murmured.

Eric smiled, acknowledging defeat. 'Until coffee time.'

He started immediately on the backlog of files on his desk, but as he worked his mind drifted back from time to time to Raymond Conroy. An attack. There would be many who would think there had been a miscarriage of justice at Newcastle Crown Court. There was a great deal of public feeling that Conroy was indeed the Zodiac Killer. But the prosecution had failed to make their case. That did not mean there might not be someone out there who would want to take the matter into his own hands. Perhaps someone had already tried.

Detective Chief Inspector Charlie Spate was late turning in at headquarters in Ponteland. He had spent the previous night with Detective Sergeant Elaine Start, and the physicality of their lovemaking had left him drained, as it often did, with a stiff back and aching loins. As a consequence he had clung to sleep, stayed in her bed after she had left, and was late rising. It was different with Elaine. Enthusiastic sex seemed to have few after effects on her. It was clear that she had greater stamina than he did, in spite of the reputation as a stud that he had built up when he was with the Met. But that was a few years ago now.

It was his reputation that had been largely responsible for his coming north: getting too close to some of the mob, and even closer with some of the girls on the game. But he had been younger then, he had to admit. And he had never met anyone quite like Detective Sergeant Elaine Start.

He had been attracted to her from the beginning, when he had first arrived on Tyneside. She had a direct look in her eye, she was smart and sassy, and she had a wicked sense of humour and great breasts. She hadn't been easy to seduce. In fact, he still wasn't sure whether it was he who achieved the seduction. He still remained unable to fathom just what made her tick. What had started for him as a slaking of lust had changed subtly over the months they had been sleeping together. He was pretty sure of his own feelings, but she consistently refused to admit to her own emotional needs as far as he was concerned. She was happy for him to visit her in her home in Westerhope from time to time, but had always refused to spend the night with him in his apartment in Wallsend. It was as though she wanted to retain control of the relationship and the situation, enjoy him on her terms and on her own territory or not at all. He resented her attitude, it affected his manly pride, but was not prepared to forego the pleasures that she provided him simply because it was she who decided upon the time and place for their lovemaking.

Apart from the stiff back, he was also irritated that, as usual, when he overslept as a result of their exertions, she never did. This morning, for instance, he had woken to find her already departed for work. And when he arrived at the office he learned from the desk sergeant she was already on duty in the interview room.

'Who's she got in there?' Charlie asked, yawning.

The sergeant looked at him contemplatively. There were rumours around headquarters about Charlie Spate and Elaine Start. Some guys got all the luck. 'Guy called Lawson.'

'What's it about?'

'Assault and battery.'

Charlie scowled. 'What the hell is she doing messing about with a piddling thing like that?'

The duty sergeant wrinkled his nose. 'ACC Charteris

heard we'd dragged the guy in last night, so detailed DS Start for it.'

'Charteris? Why the hell—'

'Because this guy Lawson, he gave none other than our friend Raymond Conroy a beating last night.' The sergeant sniffed, and wiped his nose against the back of his hand. 'Like a lot of us would have liked to do.'

'Conroy?' Charlie was taken aback. He had not been involved with the Zodiac Killer hearing, since the case had been handled by Midlands officers, but he'd heard there had been a lot of noise outside the courtroom, a demonstration in Wesley Square after Conroy had been released and the usual idiots shouting about justice and corruption in the police, taking the opportunity to throw abuse and the occasional bottle. But the violence had been contained, and nothing serious had occurred apart from a couple of broken windows in Dean Street. But now it seemed that someone had got to Conroy, the man Charlie himself was sure was the Zodiac Killer. And from the look in the eyes of the desk sergeant, he was not alone with that thought.

'And the assistant chief constable has called a conference for senior officers at midday,' the sergeant added, with a roll of his eyes.

ACC Jim Charteris loved his meetings, Charlie thought with contempt. But . . . an attack on Raymond Conroy. . . . Curious, he made his way along the corridor to the interview room. He opened the door and stepped inside. Elaine Start looked up, her eyes widening. She nodded to him and for the benefit of the recording said, 'Detective Chief Inspector Spate has entered the room. . .' She consulted her watch. 'At 10.30.'

The emphasis she placed on the time made it sound like an unspoken criticism. Charlie shrugged his shoulders and then winced, aware suddenly of the scratches her nails had left on his back last night. He glanced at the stolid-featured constable standing just inside the door. He nodded to him. 'OK, son, you can get yourself a coffee now.'

After the constable left, Charlie took a seat beside Elaine and studied the man facing them.

He was perhaps thirty years of age. He was dressed in a worn black leather jacket, jeans and heavy boots. He was burly in build; the hair on his head had been shaved closely, possibly to obviate the signs of incipient baldness, or more likely to demonstrate he was a hard man. Under his heavy, dark eyebrows his eyes were surly. He had placed his hands on the table in front of him: they were thick-fingered, clenched, his right knuckle marked with a red-raw area. His stubbly lantern jaw was set angrily and there were dark pouches under his eyes. Charlie had seen men like this often enough on the streets, men who seethed with a barely controlled rage that could burst out suddenly into a flare of violence. They often had dogs: bad-tempered, big, nasty dogs controlled only by boot or fist.

Elaine switched off the recorder and leaned back in her chair, then folded her arms over her bosom. In his imagination, Charlie could still almost feel the yielding warmth and softness of it under his cheek. 'DCI Spate, this is Mr Gary Lawson,' Elaine said. 'He's come up from the Midlands, Evesham way, with the precise intention of sorting out all our little problems for us.'

'Is that so?' Charlie replied, thrusting away memories of Elaine's flesh and staring at the man in front of him. 'And more specifically, I hear, putting his fist in the face of an innocent visitor to our area.'

Lawson's thick lips twisted in a grimace of contempt. 'Innocent? That trial was a bloody farce. It was a fix.

Everyone knows Conroy is guilty as hell! And what happens? He's shifted away from the place where we all know what went on, and he's given an easy ride by a prick of a judge who doesn't know his arse from his elbow as far as real life is concerned!'

'My, my,' Charlie murmured. 'Mr Justice Abernethy would be most interested in that view of his capabilities.' He studied Gary Lawson, observing the anger in his cold eyes. 'So, bashing Mr Conroy. Why did you feel you have to take things into your hands so personally?'

Lawson's voice was almost like a growl deep in his throat. 'That perverted bastard killed three women in the Midlands. And he terrorized a community with his sick-minded actions. He's round the bend, a lot of people say, but I reckon he's just twisted, sadistic ... look at the way he dealt with the women he abducted. Taking a scalpel, carving loony signs in their flesh—'

'You sound very certain he was the man who committed those murders,' Elaine intervened.

'It was him,' Lawson snarled.

Elaine glanced briefly at Charlie, then raised an interrogative eyebrow. 'How can you be so sure? Do you have any information, other than that brought in by the prosecution, that could lead to his conviction?'

Gary Lawson glared at her. 'I *saw* him!'

The room was suddenly very quiet. Charlie frowned, glancing at Elaine. Then he leaned forward, rubbing his thumb against his mouth. 'What do you mean, you saw him? You mean you saw Conroy in the act? That can't be so!'

'I saw him,' Lawson insisted stubbornly. 'I was supposed to meet Irene—'

'That would be Irene Dixon, one of the victims,' Elaine intervened.

'That's right. I was going to meet her, the night she disappeared. I was waiting for her outside the Green Man, near the bus stop. And I saw her. The car came past me, I saw her face, her eyes were wide and she was shouting something. He must have picked her up, offered her a lift and because she was late she accepted. That was the last time I saw her. Two weeks later they found her body.'

'You *saw* the driver?' Elaine asked, puzzled.

'I saw him.'

There was something odd about the man's insistence. Charlie stared at him. 'You say you caught a glimpse of the driver . . . and it was Conroy.'

'It was Conroy,' Lawson snarled.

'When did you tell the police about this?' Elaine asked quietly.

There was a brief hesitation. Lawson grunted, then lowered his head. 'After he was arrested.'

Charlie glanced at Elaine and raised his eyebrows. 'How long after he was arrested did you make the identification?'

'What does it matter?' Lawson snapped. 'It was after his first appearance before the magistrates. I was there. I recognized him in the courtroom. It was Conroy. I knew it. I *knew* it!'

There was a short silence. Lawson glared at his clenched fists. Charlie sighed. 'The prosecution didn't use your . . . so-called evidence.'

Lawson ran an angry hand over his shaven skull. 'They were blind, biased. They didn't believe me!'

'What about the car?' Elaine asked softly. 'Were you able to describe it?'

Lawson raised his head. Something flickered in his eyes, a wild, unreasoning fury. 'I didn't pay attention to the car! I saw her face! I recognized her. I waited, and when she didn't turn up I knew something bad had happened!'

Elaine touched her lips with her tongue. She leaned forward. 'What was your relationship with Irene Dixon?'

'We were . . . close.' Lawson frowned, fidgeted, and seemed suddenly reluctant to explain further. 'I . . . if things had been . . . we could have got married.'

'Were you going out together?' Elaine asked.

Lawson wriggled. 'We hung out in the pub, like, with mates, and. . . .' His voice died away, furiously.

'And you were to meet her that night,' Elaine pressed.

'Well, I knew she was going to be at the Green Man. There was darts going on and, well, I stood outside, waiting. . . .'

To intercept her. Chat her up. There had been no *arranged* meeting. Charlie got the picture. Like him, the Midlands officers would also have got the real scenario. Not the one churning around in Lawson's fevered imagination. Charlie had come across men like Lawson before. Inadequates in one sense, men who felt they had achieved a relationship with a woman without ever really realizing it was no more than a casual friendship. And when the possibility was taken away, the relationship would have become greater, more intimate in the man's mind, with infinite possibilities, and there would be a black rage rising, a rage that could lead to violence. The prosecution had not used Lawson because they knew his evidence was unsafe. He had probably been a mere acquaintance of Irene Dixon, and there had been no close relationship other than in his own mind. They would have realized he was a fantasist. There were certainties there in his head, but they probably never had a basis in reality.

'So you've followed this case closely,' Charlie suggested.

'I've watched that arrogant bastard all through this,' Lawson growled. 'I've watched him standing there, preening, so full of himself, and I told myself that if I ever got my hands on him, I'd tear that arrogance out of him. The things he did to Irene—'

'And you came up here to Newcastle just to follow the case.' Charlie scratched his cheek. 'Time on your hands? What do you do, Lawson? What's your job?'

Lawson lowered his head. 'I was working on a building site. I'm unemployed now. I was turned off.'

Charlie could guess why. His obsession would have overcome him. Elaine sighed. Charlie knew she was already up to speed with this. 'You were there in the courtroom when the judge threw out the case against Conroy.'

'Him, and that bloody lawyer. She thought she was so smart but it's all legal tricks. I know that bastard Conroy did it. Did it to Irene, and those other girls as well. I know it, like Jack Capaldi knows it—'

'Jack Capaldi? Who's he?' Charlie asked.

'He's Jean Capaldi's old man.'

'You've talked this over with the father of the first woman to be killed?' Elaine queried.

'Why the hell not? We had things in common! We'd both lost someone we loved. And we both know it was Conroy who used that bloody scalpel!'

Charlie rose to his feet, scraping back his chair. He was suddenly irritated. He was himself of the view that Conroy really could be the man who had killed the three women, but it was one thing to suspect, another to be as certain as the man facing them in the interview room. He walked across the room and stood against the wall, hands thrust into his pockets. Elaine glanced at him, frowned, and then continued with her questioning of Gary Lawson. She made no attempt to start the recorder again.

'So you were in court when the judge threw out the case against Conroy. How did you happen to come across him again last night?'

A confident sneer crept across Lawson's mouth. He shook his head contemptuously. 'It was no accident. I know how things work,' he snarled. 'Police, lawyers, corruption . . . you all think people like me and Jack Capaldi are stupid. It suits you to think that, doesn't it? It masks your own stupidities. It was no big deal, finding out where Conroy would hide himself, like a rat in a sewer. Capaldi and I were in court. We'd already agreed that if things went wrong, we'd work together. So while he was out front in that mob, watching what happened, I stayed away, near the back exit from the tunnel, waiting. And it was the way I'd guessed. Capaldi saw the police car out front, the decoy, but me, I saw that pair of bloody corrupt lawyers drive out with Conroy in the back of their car. It was easy enough to follow them, watch as they dropped the bloody killer at the hotel in Gosforth.'

'You must have been on foot. So how—'

'I was waiting, with my motorbike. I followed the lawyers in their car. Easy. I saw them drop Conroy at the hotel. After that, it was just a matter of waiting for the murderous bastard to show himself.'

'You waited all evening until he came out into the street.'

Lawson's mouth was hard. 'He came out. Like always. Careless. Confident. Sneering. Arrogant. But I saw the look in his eyes when I went up to him. He knew what was about to happen. And if there hadn't been other people about, shoving their noses in, I'd have cracked his bloody skull!'

Elaine looked at the notes provided by the arresting officers. Students passing by had intervened, preventing Lawson completing the assault. 'So you admit to attacking him, in an unprovoked fashion,' she stated flatly.

'Unprovoked? He was a murderer. He killed Irene, and Jean Capaldi and that other girl, and he thought he'd got away with it! I'd do it again, if he was here in front of me! I wanted to smash his face in, make him feel some of the pain Irene must have felt before she died. I wanted it to be slow, a pounding of his face, feeling his nose break, tasting the blood spraying around—'

'Like blood, do you?' Charlie asked.

Lawson glared at him in subdued fury.

'We found a knife in the bushes beside the hotel front,' Elaine said quietly.

Lawson's features stiffened as he seemed to retreat, his eyelids lowering. 'Nothing to do with me.' He hesitated. 'There was a crowd gathered straightaway. It was the wrong time to go for that bastard, I know it now. Too many people. But if I had the chance again. . . . The knife, that could have come from someone hanging around, that was nothing to do with me. I wanted my fists in his face.'

Elaine glanced at Charlie; he grimaced in distaste. The interview was taking them nowhere. He guessed there was no solicitor present because Lawson didn't want legal representation, didn't trust lawyers. He'd have form, no doubt, would know how the system worked. So what were they dealing with here anyway? Breach of the peace? Assault? They would find difficulty linking the knife to Lawson unless there was clear DNA available. And even then, it hadn't been used.

It would be up to Conroy, he thought. And if Charlie was in Conroy's shoes he wouldn't press charges. He wouldn't want further publicity. Charlie stood away from the wall, grunted, then nodded to Elaine. 'I'll send the constable in again.'

For Lawson, maybe another night in the cells and probably a warning, if Raymond Conroy pressed no charges. Even so, he wouldn't give much for Conroy's chances if Gary Lawson ever managed to catch up with him again.

Raymond Conroy needed to fade into the background, keep his head down, and hope that in the end everything would all blow over. Assuming he was not the homicidal maniac the public seemed to think he was. In which case Charlie hoped the man would clear off back to the Midlands.

Rather than seek fresh fields to conquer on Tyneside.

At the door Charlie paused. 'You got a dog, Lawson?'

Suspicion flared in the man's eyes. 'At home. Doberman.'

Charlie could have guessed.

2

Eric reached Alnwick at three in the afternoon.

He drove down to the walled town, seat of the Duke of Northumberland, and left his Celica in the small car park outside the city walls. He picked up his briefcase and strolled into the town through the fifteenth-century Hotspur Gate. He found the offices of Strudmore and Evans easily enough in Bondgate: based in a solid red-stoned building with mullioned windows in the main street, overlooking the nineteenth-century marketplace. He had never had dealings with this particular firm of lawyers but from the confident style of their offices the partnership would seem to be a relatively flourishing one. A bit of commercial work, perhaps, but more likely relying upon business undertaken for some of the landed gentry in Northumberland. Estate management could be lucrative enough, as he knew from the period he had worked for his wife. Ex-wife, he grimaced. He pushed open the door and announced himself to the receptionist. A few minutes later he found himself in an office on the first floor, overlooking the narrow gateway to the city walls. The wooden flooring creaked and groaned, proudly proclaiming its age.

Mr Strudmore was short, plump, middle-aged, self-satisfied and friendly. He was dressed in a tweed suit of some longevity as though to announce his country leanings; a somewhat flamboyant bow-tie demonstrated his confidence. His moustache was grey, neatly trimmed and contrasting in colour to the bushy red hair that sprouted above his ears. Red, fading to an odd kind of orange. Bottled youth.

He rose from behind his desk, advanced upon Eric and extended a fleshy, damp hand. 'Mr Ward. We've not met previously, but you've been pointed out to me at Law Society dinners. You used to represent and act for Morcomb estates.'

'I did. Some years ago.'

Strudmore bounced on his heels reflectively, in a curious rocking motion. 'Ah, yes . . . I've met your . . . ah . . . ex-wife, of course, on estate matters. But now you're here looking after the interests of Miss Owen.'

'Sharon has asked me to represent her, that's right,' Eric agreed.

Strudmore waved Eric to a chair and sat down himself, behind a polished desk. In front of him was a thick pile of documents, the file cover tied with pink string. He smiled. 'I'll be more than a little relieved to hand these papers over to you at long last. It's been a long-running business, the Chivers Trust.'

Eric nodded in agreement. 'Miss Owen had more or less suggested that was so.'

'Goes back three generations,' Strudmore mused, 'and it

gave rise to certain complications. Unfortunately, we weren't involved in the matter immediately, and certain mistakes were made by the previous solicitors, papers lost, that sort of thing. It was my father who sorted it out sensibly,' he added, 'when the matter was handed over to us at last. By Mr Peter Chivers.'

'I'm not at all familiar with the details of the case,' Eric admitted.

'Ah, well, perhaps I should fill you in a little before you sign for the papers,' Strudmore replied, putting the tips of his chubby fingers together. 'A coffee, while we talk?'

Eric nodded, then waited while Strudmore phoned down to his secretary. 'Now then, where was I?' Strudmore said, smiling. 'Ah, yes, the Chivers Trust.'

Eric leaned back in his chair. He had the feeling that though he would have been able to work out the details for himself by a perusal of the files, Strudmore was anxious to tell him all about it. Perhaps he had little else to do.

'Now, let me see,' Strudmore said, putting his head back on his leather chair and staring at the ceiling, 'I'll indulge myself, if you don't mind, by recalling the details without reference to the files. A good procedure, I believe, testing the memory. Don't you agree? In legal matters a good memory is important, recalling details. Yes. Right, as I recall, the trust was originally set up by one George Chivers, bypassing the interests of his son and daughter, whom he provided for separately. But let's start at the beginning.'

Eric thought that would have been the beginning. He sat back in resignation and awaited the arrival of the coffee.

'From what I've been able to ascertain, not being in possession of all the facts, George was an interesting, somewhat mysterious character. He was born about 1920 and became quite wealthy as a result of his activities in the

Second World War. Ostensibly, the wealth came from his business in the munitions industry. He never served in the armed forces, but on the other hand there were a number of unexplained absences from home during the forties and a few hints among the extant papers that would lead me to believe he was involved to some extent in intelligence activities. Be that as it may, there is no doubt he accumulated a great deal of money from his factories. Government contracts, it seems. A favoured client. As for his various *escapades*, well, they are lost in the mists of time and official fudging of details.'

Escapades. There had been a certain relish in the manner in which Strudmore had used the word. Eric had the feeling that Strudmore would have liked to know more about George Chivers and his dashing, possibly raffish existence.

'George had married quite early in life, perhaps because of the war and the feeling that all could be over very quickly. Many young people did, I understand. *Carpe diem*, you know, seize the day.' Strudmore squinted at Eric, a hint of lasciviousness in his smirk. 'Or maybe it was just animal passion. Anyway, he married Flora Denton in 1939. Their first child, Peter, was born in 1941. A second child, a daughter called Anne – that's Miss Owen's mother – was born a year later. Quite how much the children saw of their father during the war is difficult to ascertain; certainly, once the war was concluded George seems to have been very much the absentee husband. You will see from the files that by 1947 he was living and working in Scotland, in Edinburgh and Glasgow. There's nothing in the papers to suggest a formal separation or a marital breakdown, but it's clear that Flora saw little of her husband over the following years, and the children, who were in due course sent to boarding schools, lacked the guidance of a male parent in their lives.'

There was a tap on the door; a young woman with fashionably tousled hair and knowing eyes came in with the coffee. Strudmore smiled at her in a benign fashion and with an old-world courtesy personally handed Eric his coffee. As the young woman left with the empty tray, Strudmore's glance lingered almost hungrily over her swaying hips. He was silent for a little while as he sipped his coffee, then laid the cup down on his desk.

'Now, where was I? Ah, yes, Scotland. As I explained earlier there is some mystery about what George was up to in the north after the war but as far as I can make out it was something to do with the Ministry of Defence. But no matter. None of this is strictly relevant, hey?' Strudmore giggled. 'Just background matters. What is clear is that his business interests continued to flourish and by the time the children reached their majority there was certainly no shortage of money and Flora was living in some style here in Alnwick. You probably won't know the building, but it's quite a handsome Victorian mansion just off the A1 . . .' Strudmore paused, frowned slightly, picked up his coffee cup and raised it to his lips. 'She was still there in 1971 when some sort of argument arose, tore at the family. I don't know whether it occurred because of George's natural inclinations, or perhaps it was a result of marital breakdown, it's not clear, and it's all a private matter hushed up by the family anyway, but it seems George had been keeping a mistress in Glasgow. George was fifty years old by then, and his, ah, companion was at most about twenty, or twenty-two. Thereabouts. There was a flurry of letters, it would seem, because the girl – Sally Chalmers, I believe she was called – may have been in some financial difficulty. I'm not sure what it was all about because correspondence originally in the file had been weeded, at the insistence of Mrs Flora Chivers, I believe.'

Eric shifted in his chair. He suspected all this might have nothing to do with the trust; it was merely the prurient inquisitiveness of an ageing lawyer.

Strudmore put the tips of his fingers together and stared again at the ceiling. 'In a spare hour I once caused a check to be made of the local press at the time. Just as a matter of curiosity. I can't be sure it was the same person, but it seems there was a prison sentence involved. It was a sad business, really, because George died in 1973 and little more is heard of the unfortunate Sally Chalmers.'

'You say, "unfortunate"?'

Strudmore nodded. 'George Chivers was a wealthy man. He had made a will in 1958. It seems, however, that he never effected any changes to the will to take account of his liaison with Miss Chalmers.'

'I see.'

Strudmore appeared slightly disturbed and shook his head. 'Yes. Used and cast aside, I fear. Way of the world. Originally, there was a letter in the file, written by Miss Chalmers. I can't imagine what it was about. There is a reply, a sort of final letter that tells us little. You will see it for yourself. But the rest, I'm afraid it was the supporting correspondence ensuing that was later weeded out.' Strudmore's glance wavered and dropped from the ceiling, and in a slightly flustered tone, as though he realized he had been wandering, went on, 'However, I'm rambling. All this is strictly speaking nothing to do with Miss Owen and the trust fund.'

Eric sipped his coffee, relieved that perhaps they were now approaching the core of the matter.

'After the death of George Chivers, most of his money

went to his widow Flora, with legacies to the two children
Peter and Anne. George's son Peter took over the running of
the family business but soon began to diversify into
property development. He displayed a business acumen
which was certainly the equal of his father's. When his
mother Flora passed on, her estate was divided equally
between Peter and his sister Anne. However, a large part of
the estate had already been tied up in a family trust, set up
by George in favour of his grandchildren, and while Peter
was by now running his own property business successfully,
trouble arose because of the activities of Anne's husband.'

Eric was getting a little lost. 'Peter's sister Anne had
married?'

Strudmore nodded. 'The daughter of George Chivers,
Anne, married a solicitor. James Owen.'

'That would be Sharon's father.'

'Correct,' Strudmore enunciated primly. He eyed Eric
carefully for a few moments. 'It would have been better, in
my view, if the trust had been handled independently of
family, but that did not happen. James Owen, whose own
legal practice had never been particularly flourishing, took it
upon himself to administer the Chivers Trust personally.
Possibly at the suggestion of his wife Anne. Not a good idea.
I fear he was not very . . . shall we say, efficient.'

There was something in his tone that suggested more than
lack of efficiency. 'How do you mean?' Eric asked, his
curiosity at last being aroused.

'You'll be aware, naturally, that in any trust business of
any consequence there are restrictions relating to the use of
investments . . . wider range and narrower range.
Investments were made by James Owen. But when James
Owen died suddenly of a heart attack three years ago it was
discovered that he had paid little regard to these legal

restrictions. As a consequence, quite a lot of money would seem to have been dissipated. Which brings us to the crux of the problem.'

'Family dispute,' Eric sighed, and finished his coffee.

Strudmore nodded. 'My own take on the situation is that the two siblings, Peter and Anne, had never been particularly close. Perhaps because of their upbringing, with their father always away from home. Or Flora's . . . rather cool character, perhaps? Who can tell? However, the families were not really in touch with each other, quite distant even though they both lived in the north. Peter ran his property development business and his daughter Coleen was in due course made a board member.'

'Coleen would be a granddaughter of George Chivers, and therefore a beneficiary under the trust,' Eric suggested.

'That is correct, Mr Ward.'

'You haven't mentioned Peter Chivers' marriage.'

'Ah, but of course.' Strudmore seemed briefly disorientated, disturbed in his narrative. 'Yes, Peter Chivers married, but his wife died in childbirth. The daughter, Coleen Chivers, was born in 1973. Father and daughter were close; he trained her into the business. From the correspondence, and the instructions she has given to her legal representatives in the matter of the trust, she seems to be a hard, aggressive businesswoman.' He smiled faintly. 'I take no sides in this quarrel, of course.'

'The quarrel,' Eric prompted him. 'It relates to the proceeds of the trust?'

'Precisely. Coleen Chivers is now managing director of a successful property development company and one would think that she would hardly bother with such matters but she has shown a persistent interest in the . . . ah . . . black hole that appeared in trust fund moneys as a result of the depredations of James Owen.'

Perhaps the word had slipped out. Previously, Strudmore had spoken only of inefficiency. 'Depredations?' Eric asked carefully.

Strudmore sniffed, then wrinkled his nose in distaste. 'Well, yes, I'm afraid it was not simply a matter of inefficiency, but wrongdoing, I regret to say. Mr Owen had made certain drawings on the funds, to his own benefit.'

'At the same time his daughter Sharon, a beneficiary under the trust, was becoming a lawyer herself,' Eric mused.

Strudmore was silent for a little while. Thoughtfully, he said, 'Miss Owen is carving a successful career for herself at the bar. I think she comes out of all this as the only clear-sighted and sensible person in the whole business. The trust is to be wound up, she and her cousin Coleen Chivers are the sole beneficiaries, but while Miss Chivers has insisted on demanding her full rights Miss Owen has kept her distance. Leaving matters to her lawyers. You, now.' Strudmore shrugged, caressing his chubby lips with careful fingers. 'The parties haven't even met: Miss Chivers wanted action but no contact.'

'But issues have now been largely resolved?' Eric asked.

'Preliminary agreements have been drafted,' Strudmore replied, nodding. 'I would have wished that Miss Owen might have fought more strenuously for her own interests, but she has been insistent on agreeing compromises which, I must say, favour her cousin quite strongly.'

Eric could guess at Sharon's feelings: if the discrepancies had been due to her father's failings she would not have wanted to enter into bitter disputes with her cousin.

'So,' Strudmore said, tapping the files in front of him, 'I think we can safely say that all is now more or less sorted out. I have prepared the drafts; if you would like to take over

71

these files, I am happy to let you wind up the trust proper. I've taken the liberty of adding my own charges in these papers, and I must admit I'm relieved to see the end of the whole business. It's always unpleasant when families fall out.'

'Though lucrative for lawyers,' Eric added.

'Quite so.' Strudmore flushed. 'Though you will see that our charges have been reasonable, in view of the time and energy we have had to devote to this affair.'

Time, perhaps, but Eric doubted whether the chubby little partner in Strudmore and Evans would have devoted much energy to the issues. He rose, extending his hand to Strudmore. 'Good. I'll take up no more of your time. And I'm sure your charges are more than reasonable.'

Strudmore rose also, shook Eric's hand, picked up the files and presented them to him. 'And even after our charges,' he tried to joke, 'you will see that Miss Owen will receive a considerable amount of money under the trust.'

Though her cousin Coleen Chivers would get her hands on a lot more, Eric guessed.

Eric did not see Sharon that evening: she had been called away to a hearing at the Court of Appeal in London. He spent the evening at his apartment going through the trust files. It was more or less as Strudmore had explained. As a beneficiary under the Chivers Trust, Sharon would receive a considerable amount of money even though it amounted to only one third of the total. The hard-headed property developer Coleen Chivers had certainly pressed her case. With some justification, Eric was forced to admit. Sharon's father had been most indiscreet with some of the investments he had made on behalf of the trust, and there were certainly discrepancies in some of the liquid funds, discrepancies that could have caused him to be struck off the roll of solicitors had they come to light before his premature death. Eric could understand why Sharon would not want to argue too much over the splitting of the money: she would feel strongly about her father's weakness. It would be a matter of honour for her to repair the damage.

There was a brief hearing in the magistrates court to attend the following morning, after which Eric dawdled over a coffee at The Slug and Lettuce on the Quayside before presenting himself at the office again. He held a brief consultation with his two assistant solicitors concerning the immigration briefs that had come in from the Home Office and reached agreement over some of the files that were crying out for attention. He spent the rest of the morning with two clients before having a sandwich at his desk.

Susie buzzed him at three in the afternoon. 'Mr Fraser is here. Are you ready to see him now?'

'Fraser?' For a moment Eric was puzzled, then he muttered under his breath. The man he had taken for a journalist, who had spoken briefly to him at the end of Conroy's trial. He sighed. 'Yes, you can send him in, Susie.'

Some moments later the man who had introduced himself as Tony Fraser entered the room.

He was still clad in the worn leather jacket and jeans and his shirt collar was still grubby. He held out his hand: his handshake was limp, the skin soft as a woman's. He was smiling but the smile did not reach his eyes. There was something about the man Eric did not like though he was unable to pin down what it was. It might have been the air of failure that hung around the man, the feeling of disappointment that seemed ingrained in the sagging line of his jaw, the insincerity of the smile. Fraser sat down. Eric decided to dispense with the usual courtesies, and make the interview as brief as possible.

'What can I do for you, Mr Fraser?'

Tony Fraser's glance flickered around the room. 'I was very impressed, Mr Ward, by Miss Owen's handling of the case against Raymond Conroy. But, of course, she would have been well briefed by you.'

Eric remained silent.

Fraser licked dry lips. He coughed nervously. 'Perhaps I should explain. It's a few years ago that I decided to follow a career as a journalist. It's a tougher game than I expected, but I've persisted and things aren't going too badly at the moment.'

'Which newspaper are you with?' Eric asked.

There was a short silence, a hesitation as Fraser's glance flicked away from Eric and looked around the room again. 'Well, I'm sort of freelance, in that I'm not in full employment with any one newspaper, but I've had pieces in the *Metro*, and occasional articles in the *Shields Gazette*. . . .'

His voice died away uncertainly. Eric frowned. 'The *Metro* . . . that's a free newspaper, isn't it?'

'It's interested in local news, of course,' Fraser said hurriedly. 'However, I feel that my future is more to be secured in the field of rather longer pieces, if you know what I mean. I'm a great admirer of those writers who concentrated on real-life drama, like Truman Capote and his *In Cold Blood*, and the Lord knows there's enough of that sort of thing around. Which is why I felt it would be useful if I came to talk to you.'

Eric chewed his lip. 'I'm not certain quite what you mean.'

Fraser took a deep breath and forced a nervous smile to his lips. 'I've been following the Raymond Conroy case since the beginning. I mean, the actual killings, the published details . . . and then when Conroy was arrested my interest increased. Of course, the collapse of the trial has raised a number of questions, a package of issues, and I feel it would offer me the breakthrough I've been seeking.'

'Breakthrough,' Eric murmured, still unclear about Fraser's motives.

'I would like to write a book about Conroy, not seeking to brand him as a killer, if you understand what I mean, but to set his life against the background of the murders, to show how a man can be caught up by circumstance, have his life all but destroyed by rumour and innuendo, and to delve into his innermost thoughts and desires. . . . Sort of like Henry Fonda in that film about an innocent man charged—'

Eric shook his head and interrupted him. 'I'm not sure why you're talking to me about this. I don't see how I can help you.'

Fraser took a deep breath and linked his fingers tightly together. 'You've been briefed by Conroy,' he said. 'You've had opportunity to talk with him, discuss the murders, learn about his background, his feelings. . . .'

Eric held up a hand. 'I think I should stop you there, Mr Fraser. As a . . . journalist, you must surely be aware that anything I learn while acting for Mr Conroy would have been covered by the lawyer-client relationship, and could not be disclosed without the permission of the client himself.'

Hurriedly, Fraser said, 'Well, yes, but now the relationship is over, I would have thought that you would be free to talk. Not about the details relating to the case itself, because I understand your position there, but about your own take on the man, your own feelings, your view about him as a person, his motives, his—'

'I'm a lawyer, not a psychologist,' Eric interrupted quietly.

'And I fear that my own feelings or views would still fall, as far as I'm concerned, within the restriction placed by the lawyer-client relationship. Mr Conroy has spoken to me in confidence during the period that I represented him. I would have to keep that confidence. I fear I'm unable to help you, Mr Fraser.'

'You could recommend me to him,' Fraser suggested.

'I don't know what you mean.'

'You could put me in touch with him. Explain to him what I'm after. Convince him of my bona fides!'

Eric rose slowly from his seat, wandered over towards the window and took a deep breath. Fraser was irritating him with his persistence. He turned to face the man seated in front of him. 'I repeat, Mr Fraser, I don't see how I can help you. I acted as Conroy's lawyer. Nothing he told me during that period can be repeated by me without his permission. And to be frank, I would be reluctant to do that even if he gave me that permission. I'm clear about my responsibilities as a lawyer. I'm equally clear that I have no desire to get involved in the kind of project that you are considering.'

Oddly enough, Fraser did not seem surprised, or even greatly disappointed. He frowned; thought for a moment. Then he nodded. 'I understand your position, Mr Ward. Perhaps I've been ... overcome by my enthusiasm. I've pinned a lot of hopes on this idea – I feel it could be my way to success and God knows I've seen little enough of that over the years. But you see, well, I'll be frank with you. My background has been, shall we say, difficult. I was raised in a series of foster homes. I was subjected to abuse. I got in with the wrong kind of kids and I got into trouble. I'll confess to you that I've spent time in prison myself, Mr Ward, but the few years I did inside made me realize there was a better life available. It was then I decided to become a journalist. Took a correspondence course in prison. But it's turned out to be a tough choice. I've still to prove myself. But I know what it's like to be suspected, to be innocent when others say you deserve conviction. I'm drawn to Raymond Conroy. He's had a tough deal. He has a story to tell.' His eyes were fixed on Eric, earnestly. 'And with my experience, I think I'm the man to tell it to the world.'

He saw the determination in Eric's eyes and he hurried on. 'But I accept you can't help me in the manner I would have wished. On the other hand, if you would be prepared just to put me directly in touch with Conroy. Perhaps explain what I'm after. Persuade him—'

Eric shook his head. 'I'm afraid I can't even do that, Mr Fraser.'

'But at least you must know where he's to be found at the moment!'

Eric hesitated. It was already public knowledge that there had been a fracas outside the hotel in Gosforth. Fraser should follow his own nose on the matter. Eric could suggest to him that he might follow the trail from the hotel. Then he demurred once again. 'I'm sorry, Mr Fraser. Conroy is still my client at the moment, though that relationship is about to end. I regret I really can't help you.'

He moved towards the door and opened it. He could have offered Fraser a lifeline, the hope that he might succeed in his enterprise. But he could not bring himself to do it. Raymond Conroy had been charged with murder, had faced trial, had escaped conviction for the moment – the last thing he would want would be to be pursued by an obsessive who wanted to write his life story, peel back his emotional skin to determine his innermost feelings. A journalist with his own life problems.

Disappointed or not, Fraser was not someone to whom

Eric owed a thing, and he had no intention of getting involved with a man who was seeking to make his own reputation by dredging into the sensationalism that had already surrounded the hunt for the Zodiac Killer. Fraser did not say goodbye as he left. He failed to meet Eric's eyes. There was disappointment in the set of his shoulders as he made his way through Susie's office. Eric closed the door on him with relief.

Shaking his head, he picked up the phone and dialled Sharon's chambers. After a brief conversation with the clerk, he was put through to her extension.

'Hi. Look, I've been up to Alnwick and I've met the solicitor who was holding the papers. Strudmore. You met him?'

'Damp hands, eye for the ladies.'

Eric laughed. 'That's him. Anyway, he insisted on giving me the family history as well as the trust papers. Seems to me the papers at least are all in order. Your family . . . that's another matter.'

'Tell me about it,' Sharon laughed.

'Anyway, all I need to do is get your final written consent to the distribution of the funds in the trust. Can we get together to do that?'

'Very businesslike,' she laughed.

'Doesn't stop us having dinner afterwards,' he suggested.

'Instead of a fee?'

'That's a deal.'

He had barely replaced the phone when Susie Cartwright tapped at the door and entered. She closed it behind her. There was a strange look on her face. Her lips were tight with disapproval. Eric raised his eyebrows. 'A problem?'

'There's someone in reception who wants to see you.'

'So?'

'It's Raymond Conroy.'

Eric grimaced. He was silent for a moment. 'Have you sent him the bill for our fees?'

Susie nodded. 'And he's just given me a cheque.'

'Very prompt,' Eric murmured.

'And now he wants to see you.'

Hopefully, to say goodbye, Eric thought. He nodded. 'All right. Tell him I'm busy, but can spare him just a few minutes.'

Susie turned, and as she did so he recalled that Conroy had been attacked. It was possible he would want to ask Eric to start proceedings against the man who had attacked him. It was not an action Eric was keen to get involved in. A few moments later the door opened again and Raymond Conroy entered the room.

His left eye was half closed. There was a purple bruise on his forehead and his mouth was swollen. The injuries were superficial, Eric guessed, with nothing broken, but the man would have suffered a degree of pain in the fracas outside the hotel. Eric noted Conroy was also limping: his guess was that his former client may have been kicked in the leg.

'I've paid your bill, Mr Ward,' Conroy said, and his tongue flickered against his swollen lip as though it pained him to speak. 'But you will see I have been somewhat in the wars. Now, I'd like to take your advice. Regarding this assault.'

Eric did not suggest that the man sat down. He stared at Conroy, considering his words carefully. 'Mr Conroy, I have to tell you I've a great deal on my plate at the moment. Now you've paid the fees, strictly speaking our association is at an end, and you're no longer my client. If you wish to take action regarding this attack upon you, I would advise that perhaps it would be as well if you were to go to another lawyer. . . .'

His voice died away as he saw the cynical glint in Conroy's eyes.

'I merely seek a piece of simple advice, Mr Ward,' Conroy said with difficulty. 'We've got over the big problem, with your assistance ... and that of Miss Owen, of course. But now that I've been attacked—'

'If you're thinking of pressing charges,' Eric cut in, 'you should consider the consequences. If I may speak plainly, you'd be well advised to do nothing about it. You've been injured, but it doesn't seem the injuries are serious. It might be galling to you, but you must be aware that in the community at large there is a great deal of ill feeling towards you, probably stirred up by the media, but nevertheless, you should think carefully before you consider entering a courtroom again. If you were to proceed, your injuries ... well, I would suspect you'd get little by way of compensation, and as for the man who attacked you. . . .'

'He'd be regarded as a hero?' Conroy's tone had a bitter, mocking edge. 'Man attacks the freed Zodiac Killer. The alleged, falsely accused, *innocent* suspect. Justice is not available to all, it seems.'

'I would agree,' Eric replied coldly. 'The public would hold the view that there are three unfortunate women who have not yet managed to achieve justice.'

'And I remain condemned in the public consciousness even though I've been shown to be innocent of any crimes?' Conroy said challengingly.

'Even so.' Eric hesitated. 'I'm not saying you should not pursue this man for the attack upon you, but I do counsel care. You've been in the spotlight for months. You've read what's been written about you; you'll be aware of the strength of public feeling aroused by the judge throwing out the case against you—'

'Because there wasn't one!' Conroy intervened in measured, steely tones.

'The question is,' Eric continued quietly, 'do you want to inflame things further? If you bring an action against this man—'

'His name's Lawson. He was involved with one of the dead women. Or at least,' Conroy sneered, 'he claims to have been.'

'So he'll gain some sympathy in the public mind. I would tread carefully, Mr Conroy. And in view of my advice, I regret I would not wish to represent you if you wanted to take action. That doesn't prevent you going elsewhere for representation.'

There was a short silence. Raymond Conroy's good eye held Eric's for several seconds; there was a glint of understanding in the glance. At last the man nodded coldly. 'I thought that might be your advice . . . and your reaction. It's advice I am prepared to accept. You're right, of course. It would be foolish to court publicity. I've no desire to face the media pack again. I shall now seek a quiet life. But . . . I was going to ask you to do one more thing for me. However, in view of your feelings, I'll seek assistance elsewhere. You see, Mr Ward, I've decided not to return to the Midlands.'

Eric was barely surprised. Conroy would find it difficult to keep a low profile in Birmingham after what had happened, not least since no further killings had occurred during the time he had been held pending trial. 'So what will you do?'

Conroy's mouth twisted into a mockery of a smile. He glanced out of the window, nodding towards the Quayside and the river. 'The Midlands hold no attraction for me. I've put my apartment on the market. I have some private income which enables me to keep my head above water:

indulgent, wealthy, dear departed parents,' he mocked. 'How could one have gone on without them?' He waved towards the window. 'My presence here had been forced on me, of course, but I've now become quite enamoured of the far north. The decay of industry, the collapse of shipyards, the dark gleam of the river, the area offers me scope for my work, my painting. And I'm told the Northumbrian countryside is quite beautiful, and empty. Peaceful. That's what I crave now, Mr Ward. Peace. So, I came to see you to pay your fees but also to ask you to find a little property for me – a cottage, perhaps, in the country.'

Eric hesitated, opened his mouth to speak but was forestalled.

Conroy held up a hand. 'But I understand. You don't wish our acquaintance to be continued. I'm not surprised. I know you don't like me, Mr Ward.' The cold eyes held a glint of faint amusement. 'It's of little consequence. And the cottage . . . I can always see to that myself. Find some other agent, perhaps.' He stepped a little closer to Eric. 'So this can be by way of an *au revoir*.'

Eric was relieved to hear it. He moved away, not wishing to shake the man's hand.

Conroy turned, walked away, then hesitated at the door. 'I won't thank you for what you've done,' he continued, speaking with difficulty as he caressed his swollen lips. 'After all, you were simply doing your job. Efficiently, I'll admit. Though, of course, the prosecution case was a weak one . . . and I was innocent of the charges they brought.'

Eric had a crawling feeling along his spine. He had acted for Raymond Conroy, done his best to expose the weakness in the prosecution case, but he felt no great confidence that the man facing him was indeed innocent of the murders of the three women in the Midlands. And he detected a certain triumphalism in Conroy's tone, a hint of mockery as though the man felt he had won a prize, overcome his detractors.

When the door closed behind Conroy, Eric waited, and then left his office, passed a silent Susie in the anteroom and went along the corridor to the bathroom. There he washed his hands with care and rinsed his face. He stared into the mirror, observing the greying of his hair, the lines in his lean features, the settled grimness of his mouth.

He still felt grubby, unclean for having acted successfully for the man who, with his help, had probably escaped responsibility for the brutal murders of three young women. He washed his hands again, angrily, but suspected that it would be a long while before he would be able to clear his mind of guilt.

CHAPTER THREE

1

Assistant Chief Constable Jim Charteris was sharply dressed, as always. His uniform was immaculate, his shirt crisply white, his closely shaven features appropriately hawkish and his greying hair smartly arranged. His eyes were alert, his back stiff, everything about him was to attention. Charlie Spate always felt, when he saw Charteris, that the senior officer was expecting to be interviewed for promotion at any given moment. Charlie was aware that the ambitions of the assistant chief constable were as carefully honed as his appearance: the man did not intend staying too long in the north and would be seeking an early move to a more senior position, preferably in the south, which accounted for the driven fastidiousness with which he approached his work and the whip he regularly cracked over officers like Charlie, whom he regarded as insufficiently respectful of authority, even louche to a certain degree.

As he took his seat in the crowded briefing room, Charlie sighed. He had to admit that he had nursed certain ambitions of his own once, but he had lacked the ferociously egocentric drive that Charteris displayed. As a young officer Charlie's investigative talents had been recognized and he had obtained promotion in the Met. The temptations, however, were too numerous: accepting some of the invitations presented on a plate to him in the Soho area had finally led to an internal enquiry which, while failing to demonstrate that there had been a dereliction of duty on his part, or any financial corruption, had nevertheless come to the conclusion that he would be better employed elsewhere. Hence, a transfer to the north-east.

There were temptations enough on Tyneside, of course, and he had succumbed to one or two, but now that he had attached himself to DS Elaine Start his libido was more than satisfied. Charteris also would have liked to get into Elaine's knickers, Charlie suspected, but the ACC's ambition overrode his sexual leanings. As for Charlie, he was happy enough with his rank as detective chief inspector and his location in Elaine Start's bed. Occasionally. When she dictated.

He glanced along the rows of officers seated in the briefing room. DS Elaine Start was at the end of the row in front of him. He felt she was aware that his eyes were on her, but she did not turn her head. A controlled woman, he considered.

Except in bed.

ACC Charteris cleared his throat loudly. 'I would like first to introduce to you all Assistant Chief Constable Rawlins, who has hitherto led the hunt for the Zodiac Killer in the Midlands. As you will all be aware, the trial of the man charged with the killings was transferred to Newcastle to avoid the prejudice of public feeling in Birmingham. You will also be aware of the manner in which that trial collapsed.'

Charteris paused as a low, rumbling murmur of discontent ran around the room. He waited, his handsome features set grimly. When silence fell, he continued. 'I thought it would be a good idea if we held this conference this morning with ACC Rawlins in attendance, in order that he may give us the benefit of his views about the man Raymond Conroy. But first, I will allude to the incident that occurred a few days ago in Gosforth, when Conroy was attacked outside his hotel.' He smoothed a hand over his slicked-back, greying hair and bared his teeth in a grimace of distaste. 'The assailant in question is known, I understand, to ACC Rawlins. His name is Gary Lawson, a bit of a fantasist who claimed he was involved with one of the dead women, and he was investigated by our colleagues in the Midlands at the time. His attack upon Conroy in Gosforth was motivated, he claimed, by a desire to obtain the kind of justice against Conroy that the law had failed to administer. He wanted to give him a good kicking—'

'He's not alone in that,' a burly officer along the row from Charlie Spate muttered.

Charteris caught the comment but made no response to it. 'Lawson was arrested at the scene, brought in, questioned, and given a warning.'

'Should have been a medal,' another officer chimed in from the back of the room.

This time, Charteris glared at the officer concerned. He did not like being interrupted. 'Lawson has now been released. It seems that Raymond Conroy will not be pressing charges against Lawson, and it's felt that it would not be in the public interest for us to commence proceedings ourselves. Lawson has been warned, told to go back to Evesham, where he is located, and stay out of trouble. He should not get further involved in the life of Raymond

Conroy.' Charteris paused, then glanced at the man seated beside him. 'But perhaps ACC Rawlins would like to take over at this point.'

Rawlins was perhaps fifty years of age. The pouches beneath his eyes were dark, as though he had suffered too many sleepless nights. His shoulders were broad but slumped, and there were signs of deep-seated dissatisfaction about his mouth. Charlie Spate had the impression the man would be seeking retirement soon, disillusioned by his experiences in the police force, perhaps broken by the final straw supplied by the court's decision in the case of Raymond Conroy. The man would have invested a considerable amount of his time to the affair. When Rawlins spoke there was a furred edge to his voice, a chronic smoker's hoarseness, but his tone also was scarred with disappointment.

'Yes, thank you, Jim. Gary Lawson ... he's known to us. He's no angel, bit of a tearaway, has a few convictions for minor offences, and is known to be quick to use his fists or boots. Conroy was lucky Lawson got pulled away in time by bystanders, but it might not be the last time he'll come across Lawson. The man is bitter about the killing of Irene Dixon, whom he considered as a girlfriend, though there's little evidence she held him in high regard. But chances are, Lawson's not given up. He's displayed a certain obsessiveness about the death of Irene Dixon. He may well want to bring harm to the man he believes is the Zodiac Killer again. But, of course, he's not alone in making threats.'

Rawlins paused and flicked a glance around the room of silent officers. 'There's also the family of the Capaldi woman. The father, Jack Capaldi, was in court when Conroy was released from custody. He also turned up at preliminary hearings. He's issued a number of threats, and he means what he says. Another thing you need to know: Jack Capaldi also has form. Some years ago he was involved in a long-running turf war in the West Midlands over ice-cream concessions and off-course bookie shops. He won the battle. Only after a certain amount of blood was spilled.' His mouth twisted cynically. 'Not that the victims appealed to us for help. That side of the business has since been handed over to his nephew, Nick, who's another hard case. Jack Capaldi now concentrates on running small pizza businesses. Legit, as far as we know. But the family is close knit, and not afraid to stick up for what they see as due to them. In short, we're aware the Capaldi family has access to a considerable amount of muscle. The guy who murdered Capaldi's daughter was dealing with the wrong kind of family. Jack Capaldi will want revenge. And he'll go for it. Raymond Conroy needs to be careful.'

There was a short silence. Charlie broke it with a question. 'You seem pretty convinced that this Conroy character really was the Zodiac Killer.'

'*Is*,' Rawlins insisted with a grunt. He glanced at ACC Charteris. 'The team that has been pursuing this case in the Midlands, we're all convinced we got our hands on the right man. But . . . Jim here will know what it's like, the kind of political pressure that gets put on senior officers to get a result, quickly, when the public starts screaming about keeping the streets safe for women. Over a period of six months, three women were horribly tortured and murdered. The nature of the torture, well, it fascinated the media. The killer had carved a sign of the Zodiac on the breasts of each victim. In the view of the press, at least, that means he intends killing at least nine more women if he gets the chance.'

Rawlins leaned back in his chair, glowering at his

memories. 'In our patch the heat was on. Local and national press; the Home Secretary; questions in parliament. Television appeals. We got it all. We put extra men and women in the field. And we found our man. But, naturally, we had to build a cast-iron case against him, and that's where we got hustled by the politicians into acting before we had it all sewn up.'

'But you must have felt you had enough evidence to bring him to trial,' Charlie said.

'And the CPS agreed,' Rawlins countered. 'But in the end. . . . Look, the facts were like this. We trawled the area for weeks, even before the third murder. We'd worked out the killer's likely stamping ground, with the help of forensic psychologists and good police work. And we placed several officers, DS Paula Gray included, under cover. It worked. Conroy struck up an acquaintance with her. She fed him the right questions. And she got incriminating answers. The trouble was, the CPS advised us that there was too much of the honey trap in the situation and we were restricted in the evidence she was permitted to give. And . . . well, maybe she went too far.'

'Sleeping with the guy?' someone called out.

Rawlins reddened. 'She denies that. Conroy came up with the suggestion to his lawyer and the court went along with it. But it was a lie.' He paused, then nodded. 'The fact is we *had* him. But it was the last few nails in the coffin that we were missing. He fitted the profile: he wandered regularly in the area; he picked up women; he had this artistic bent. We even had the scalpel he used. . . .' He paused, recollecting the humiliation suffered by the prosecution in the courtroom when the scalpel evidence was thrown out as inadmissible. 'But what we lacked was a DNA link to the bodies.' He sighed; shook his head. 'There had to be a safe house somewhere. The women were tortured and killed some place he had access to, used regularly, that's what we surmise. But we couldn't locate it. And after the women were dead he cleaned them up, dumped them in different locations. And he never raped them. He got his kicks from the carving, and the screams, we guess. We hunted for the torture place; we're still combing the area for it. But so far we've not found it. Sure, we know it wasn't his apartment. We guess he had access to some other place, where he did the business that turned him on. But we still haven't found it. Believe me, we'll get there eventually. We should have waited; kept the heat on him till he cracked. But he's an arrogant, self-confident bastard. He's not easy to break. And the pressure was on, from the media, from the Home Office, from the politicians. So we went with what we had.' He shrugged despondently. 'It wasn't enough.'

There was a short silence. ACC Charteris leaned forward. He frowned; glanced around the room. 'And that's where we are today. Except things have moved on somewhat. ACC Rawlins has handed over a mass of files to me. Because now *we're* involved.'

There was a rustle of movement among the officers in the room, a quickly suppressed murmur. Charteris held up an admonitory hand. 'We're now being called upon to work hand in hand with the team led by my colleague here. ACC Rawlins and his team will continue to follow up all possible leads in the Midlands to find out exactly where the murders – and the tortures – were carried out. As for us, we'll be keeping a close eye on Raymond Conroy . . . who, as far as we're concerned, is the man still in the frame. In spite of the collapse of the trial.'

Charlie Spate raised his head. 'I'm not clear about this, sir. What's going on?'

Rawlins leaned forward again and passed a hand over his tired eyes. 'It seems Raymond Conroy's put up his apartment for sale. And the property has been snapped up. There are always ghouls who'll want to buy a place connected to a celebrity ... and Conroy's got celebrity status, believe me, even if it is of a ghastly kind.'

Charteris nodded grimly in agreement. 'And from what we hear, Raymond Conroy intends relocating up here. We've been keeping tabs on him at his hotel, but he's now moved out, and is renting a terraced house in Gosforth. But it's a short-term let. It looks as though he's consulting estate agents, looking for some place to buy. In other words, the man who we think killed those women, the Zodiac Killer as the press have dubbed him, is going to be living in the north-east. So he's now becoming our responsibility. And I want that responsibility taken seriously.'

There was a general shifting of bodies, a swelling murmur of conversation. ACC Charteris waited for a little while, then raised his hand for silence. 'Our colleagues in the West Midlands were working from scratch: they had no idea who they were looking for originally. It's different for us. As a result of the investigations carried out by ACC Rawlins' team, we've got a mass of information about Raymond Conroy now: we know his likes, his habits, his *modus operandi*. And it's my intention that we make life hell for him. We put pressure on the bastard. We keep him under strict surveillance. We let him know we're watching him. At the least we'll make sure he doesn't use a scalpel on any women up here. And at best. . . .' He glanced sideways at the lowered head of ACC Rawlins. 'At best we'll make him crack, make a mistake, take one chance too many and we'll *get* him.'

Charlie Spate was aware of the tide of approval that

washed through the room. He had some doubts himself: putting pressure on Conroy was well enough, but the man had already shown he had an arrogant resistance to such pressure. The surveillance could be a long job.

'So, from today,' ACC Charteris was saying, 'new schedules will be raised. I'm approving extra overtime arrangements. There'll be round-the-clock surveillance. I want to see DCI Spate in my office after this meeting: he will be acting in a co-ordinating role and will oversee the group.'

His glance flickered briefly in Charlie's direction. 'He'll be able to show us what he learned in the Met before he came to give us the benefit of his experience up here.'

Charlie was aware of the sourness of the jibe: Charteris and he had never got on well together. He sighed. He had the despairing feeling that this was going to be a question of supping with the devil. With a spoon that would be barely long enough.

2

It was several days before Eric was able to arrange a meeting with Sharon Owen: she had been working on yet another case at the Court of Appeal in London and although they had spoken a few times on the phone, he had been unable to obtain her signature to the documents he was holding on her behalf.

The wait gave him opportunity to spend more time on the file. Strictly speaking, all that really concerned him was the agreement that Strudmore had raised on behalf of the trust with Sharon's cousin Coleen. He had checked them carefully against the trust documents and all seemed in order, but he was a little curious as to why Sharon's cousin Coleen

Chivers seemed to have insisted on receiving the lion's share of the trust funds. Of course, it was Sharon's father, the solicitor James Owen, who had caused the value of the trust to be diminished – and that was the main reason, he guessed, why Coleen Chivers had been so insistent in the negotiations. Even so, it was a family matter, and he hoped it could be resolved without too much bitterness.

Back at his apartment he opened up his laptop. He poured himself a drink and trawled the internet: he quickly turned up the website for Chivers Properties Limited. The company had been formed by Coleen's father Peter when he was in his early forties, financed no doubt by the money he had obtained at the death of his father George Chivers. As Eric recalled, after the death of George's wife Flora, the estate had been divided between Peter and his sister Anne, Sharon's mother. While some of Anne's share had been frittered away by her husband's depredations, Peter Chivers had put his share to good use. Chivers Properties Limited had grown significantly during the last forty years and held an extensive range of real estate, ranging from office blocks to industrial premises. It was now headed by Coleen Chivers, as chief executive.

Curiously, Eric switched his way through the links on the website until he came to a profile of Coleen Chivers. There was a series of photographs displayed. One of them showed her at a reception in the Mandarin Hotel in Singapore: a tall, confident, blonde woman in a low-cut evening dress, standing with some Asian men in dinner jackets. Another had been taken recently: her wind-blown hair floated about her cheeks and she was laughing, one hand on the tiller of a yacht. Eric looked carefully at the background: from the architecture of the blocks of flats he could see behind her he guessed the photograph had been taken at the marina at

Royal Quays. So she would have a boat moored on the Tyne. Something expensive, no doubt. He studied her features. She bore no resemblance to Sharon Owen, her cousin, but she was a beautiful woman. And a successful one, chief executive of a big company, wealthy ... and hard, if the negotiations over the trust money were anything to go by. Eric sipped his drink, thinking about it. Maybe it had been her lawyers. But he had no doubt Coleen Chivers was a formidable businesswoman. She'd have to be, to hold her empire together.

Legal advisers, pushing her to screw the last penny out of the trust, or maybe it had been her own toughness, based on resentment, perhaps. A family feud? They could give rise to the worst kind of battles.

He followed through on the links on the website. There was a description of the holdings of the company, the names of board members, including a titled non-executive director, and details of Coleen Chivers herself. She was thirty-six years old, he read, almost a decade older than Sharon. She had moved straight from a finishing school in Switzerland to work for her father in Chivers Properties Limited and after successfully managing a subsidiary company had been taken on to the main board under her father's chairmanship. On his death she had become chief executive and also taken his chair. The company had continued to grow, not least with some overseas acquisitions and partners.

Eric switched to the financial reports filed by the company. He scanned the figures thoughtfully. They were impressive. He wondered what the off-balance sheet figures might disclose, but certainly it seemed that the audited accounts disclosed a healthy series of operations and a steady growth of capital and revenue.

There was another photograph of Coleen Chivers

attached to the annual report. He studied it for a little while. It was quite different from the carefree shot of her on the yacht at Royal Quays. She was staring at the camera with a certain intensity. She looked older, there were lines around her eyes and mouth, and he felt it demonstrated a certain hardness about her. The jut of the jaw suggested determination; the glance held a hint of steel. It might have been a deliberate attempt to show her as the strong-minded executive she clearly was; it might, on the other hand, expose her real self, in a way the smiling images at the Singapore dinner and the yacht did not.

It was interesting, but not really relevant, after all. The negotiations had been concluded, Sharon and her cousin had agreed upon the disbursements to be made under the trust set up by George Chivers all those years ago, and all that was required was that the final documents be signed.

'So have you ever met your cousin?' Eric asked, when he finally managed to get to see Sharon.

On her return to the north, after the successful prosecution of the case to the Court of Appeal, Eric had invited Sharon to call at the flat. He had brought in some excellent Montepulciano, spent some time in the kitchen cooking a simple meal, rouget and salmon with potatoes in a cream sauce, and persuaded her that it would be a good idea if she stayed the night. She took little persuading: they had not seen each other for over a week. Then, seated side by side on the settee, with a bottle of brandy on the low table in front of them, Eric brought up the matter of the documentation to be signed, and the nature of Coleen Chivers.

'Met her?' Sharon shook her head. 'My mother was never very close to her brother Peter – Coleen's father. I think there was a certain tension between them.'

'Because of your father's handling of the trust funds?' Eric queried.

Sharon sipped at her brandy and nestled against Eric's arm. '*Mishandling*, you mean. No, I think it predated all that affair. My mother never explained in any kind of detail what it was all about, but the two of them had fallen out before my grandfather died.'

'George Chivers.'

'That's right. The source of the family's wealth. In fact, the only hint I ever got from my mother was that it was something to do with George that had caused her and her brother Peter to have a quarrel.' She wrinkled her nose. 'She told me once or twice that Peter was a bit of a tightwad. You know, he wasn't kindly inclined towards charitable causes. But I suppose that's how he became a successful businessman.'

'And was followed along that track by his own daughter, Coleen.'

Sharon glanced at him and smiled. 'You think I've given up too easily on my share of the trust fund, don't you?'

Eric shrugged. 'Not my business,' he replied. 'But had I been Strudmore, had I been advising you, I'd have held out for a fairer distribution of the proceeds of the trust. The conditions were quite clear—'

'But it was my father who had dipped his sticky fingers into trust money,' she reminded him.

'And you feel a moral obligation to recognize that in the distribution of the trust funds.'

'Exactly.' Sharon was silent for a little while, then she murmured, 'It's also a case of trying to deny my genes, I suppose.'

Eric was puzzled. 'I don't follow.'

She sighed, leaned a little closer to him. 'Look, I'm old

enough to be able to see things in a clear light, unaffected by sentimentality. Let's look at facts. Take my mother, Anne Chivers. She had a ruthless streak in her. She insisted on marrying my father James Owen in spite of parental opposition. And it was she who was determined that I should become a lawyer, read for the bar. As for my father's depredations into trust funds, I have a strong suspicion my mother knew about it, did nothing to prevent him, indeed may have supported his activities at least tacitly because she saw it as a way of getting something over her brother Peter. I suspect also she was encouraging my wayward father so that I would end up with a larger part of the trust funds, though in that she was frustrated because my father frittered away the money he had embezzled. Unsound investments.'

'Like the race track.'

She grunted in acquiescence. 'Among other things. Anyway, there's my mother. And then there was her brother Peter, the founder of Chivers Properties Limited. According to my mother he was as tight-fisted as could be. And ruthless in his pursuit of money. And women also, it seems. But, of course, in that he wasn't so far different from his father, my grandfather, old George.'

Eric shifted in his seat and stroked her hair. 'Your grandfather played around? How do you know that?'

'Family gossip,' Sharon replied, smiling. 'And, well, there's some documentation also. You've been through all the papers in the file Strudmore handed to you?'

Eric shrugged. 'Relating to the trust fund, yes. I didn't plough through the earlier papers, however, involving the years before the establishment of the trust fund.'

Sharon giggled a little guiltily. 'Well, let's take a look and you'll see what I mean. After all, you used the documents as an excuse to bring me here and have your wicked way with me, didn't you? So let's at least play fair and look at them, before you take me to bed.'

'All unwillingly.'

'But of course. And more than a little sloshed.'

Eric removed his arm, set down his brandy glass and walked across to the desk in the corner of the sitting room. He extracted the file from the drawer, glanced at it briefly and then brought it across to the settee. As he sat down beside Sharon once more she said, 'By the way, I had an odd letter waiting for me when I got back from London.'

'About this file?' he asked.

'No, no, nothing to do with that. It was about Raymond Conroy.'

'As far as I'm concerned, I'm happy to see the back of him,' Eric muttered.

'You're not alone in that. But this letter . . . it was a request for an interview. From a journalist. He wants to discuss Raymond Conroy. I haven't replied to it yet because I'm not sure I even want to think about that cold-hearted bastard, but it was such an odd proposal—'

'Was it written by a guy called Tony Fraser?' Eric asked, after a moment's thought.

'You've had one too?' Sharon queried in surprise.

Eric shook his head. 'No, I actually had a visit from the man.'

'So what's it all about? Is he some kind of ghoul, or what?'

Eric thought about it for a few moments before he answered. 'It's difficult to say, really. Fraser spoke to me at the end of Conroy's trial, and then later, while you were in London, he visited me at my office. He wanted me to tell him what I thought about Conroy, what in my view made the man tick . . . and, I suppose, he was leading up to asking me directly whether I thought Raymond Conroy really was the Zodiac Killer. I gave him little satisfaction. I imagine that's why he then wrote to you.'

'So what's he after?'

Eric sipped thoughtfully at his brandy. 'Well, as I said, as far as I could make out he wanted me to provide him with a kind of inside story on Raymond Conroy. He wanted to know what I could tell him about the man himself, his drives, his psychological make-up, how he had reacted to the charges against him. I sent him away with a flea in his ear. Told him the rules about lawyer-client relationships. As no doubt you'll do if you write to him.'

'I certainly shan't agree to meet him,' Sharon said fervently. 'But I wonder why this man Fraser would want such information anyway.'

'I got the impression,' Eric said slowly, 'that Fraser sees Conroy as a kind of lifeline, or a ladder, an opportunity that might turn out to be golden.'

'I don't follow you.'

Eric sighed. 'If you saw him, you might understand. He seems to me to be sort of . . . unfulfilled, if you know what I mean. He told me he's a journalist, but when I questioned him about that he sort of hedged. He said he was mainly freelance; admitted to writing for the *Metro*, which is a free newspaper and hardly in the top flight of daily newssheets, and other local journals. I gathered that he was probably scratching a living at journalism, little more. He would be unhappy about that. I think he's the kind of man who would feel he deserved more recognition, and was hungering to get into the big time. Make a reputation for himself. Perhaps on the back of Raymond Conroy . . . who, you have to admit, is a prime case for investigative reporting.'

'Whether he's the Zodiac Killer or not.' Sharon shivered, leaned closer to Eric. 'He's a cold-hearted, unemotional bastard, that's for sure. And you think Fraser wants to use him as a study, for an article or something? But what makes Fraser think he would be able to get close enough to Conroy to be able to produce something worthwhile?'

Eric caressed her hair with his free hand, then sipped at his brandy. 'He also told me that he himself has spent time inside, so he has some fellow-feeling for Conroy, knows the kinds of pressure that can be felt by an innocent man banged up in jail. Maybe he believes that would be enough to get close to him. But first he had to find out where Conroy was staying. That's where I came in.'

'So what are you trying to say?' she asked curiously. 'This man Fraser is a nutcase?'

Eric nodded. 'I got the impression Tony Fraser is a failure as a journalist. Maybe he's always been a failure, I don't know. But he's a sad, needy character who thinks life has treated him badly and now believes he's found a way to haul himself up by his boot straps.'

'By way of Raymond Conroy?'

'Looks like it,' Eric suggested. 'He seems to feel that if he can get inside the mind of Raymond Conroy, or at least discover what our views of the man might be—'

'As confidential counsel,' Sharon murmured.

'Then he might produce a worthwhile piece of writing, make his name as a journalist, come up with sensational discoveries, become a new Truman Capote—'

'Who?'

Eric smiled. 'You've had a sadly neglected literary experience. I'm talking about *In Cold Blood*. Never mind. But there have been hugely successful pieces of docufiction written in collaboration with killers. People have a fascination about learning the ins and outs of a killer's mind.'

'Raymond Conroy isn't a *proven* killer,' Sharon reminded him. 'We got him off, remember?'

'But there are lots of people out there who believe the police got the right man, and that Conroy really is the Zodiac Killer.'

'And this Fraser guy wants to cash in on that,' Sharon suggested.

Eric hesitated. 'Well, yes, but I think it's more than cash, more than just money. Listening to him, watching him, I wondered whether it's not so much cash as perhaps fame, or really, more importantly, self-belief.'

'He wants to write a book about Conroy?'

Eric shrugged. 'A book. Articles. I don't know. We didn't get all that far in our discussion. He wanted me to tell him where Conroy was hanging out. I refused to give him any information about it. And the letter to you—'

'I shan't answer it,' Sharon said firmly. She snuggled more closely against Eric's shoulder. 'Anyway, let's get back to my family file. I want to show you something that's linked to the adventurous and mysterious life of my grandfather, George Chivers.'

She put down her brandy glass and took the file from him. She riffled through the papers, discarding the later information relating to the trust funds and turned up some affidavits and legal documents from the 1970s. 'This is about the time grandfather George set up the trust in favour of his putative grandchildren. Me and Coleen Chivers, as it turned out.'

Eric frowned. 'Yes, I'd wondered about that. George Chivers had set up a successful business. When he died, he left a considerable amount of money to his two children, Peter and Anne Chivers. But he also set up a trust fund for his grandchildren. Now, I'll admit that kind of provision is not exactly unusual, but was there any particular reason why he should establish separate funds for his children and grandchildren?'

Sharon snorted. 'Family quarrels, what else?'

'About what?'

'That's where there's a bit of a mystery. Old George died in 1980. His estate was split between Peter and Anne, his children, with provisions for his widow Flora, including some lifetime settlements. My own mother would never talk about it, but it seems Flora and George were at loggerheads during his last years, that Peter got involved, and tempers rose to such an extent that George made a new will, and also set up the trust fund for me and Coleen. I never saw much of my granddad – he was still spending a lot of time in Scotland at that period – and I just wasn't around when the quarrels broke out. And my mother kept schtum about it all. I have often wondered since, however, whether it had something to do with what George was doing in Scotland during those years. I know he'd established some light industry up there, a paper mill or something like that, but I've also received the impression – from where I can't tell you, family chat or what – that he was also involved in some cloak-and-dagger stuff. You know, government hush-hush activity. The kind of thing that doesn't get talked about.'

'And you've no idea. . . ?'

Sharon shrugged, brushing away a lock of blonde hair from her eyes. 'I don't know. I've never been particularly interested in the political situation in the seventies. But this is what I wanted you to see.' She extracted a sheet of paper from the file. 'It's all rather inconclusive, since it looks to me as though earlier correspondence has been weeded from the file.'

Eric recalled his conversation with the family lawyer

Strudmore. The solicitor had suggested letters certainly had been taken out of the file concerning George Chivers' romantic activities in Scotland. 'And you think it was in some way security related?'

'Uh-huh. I've got a feeling about it. Or maybe it was whispers around when I was a child. Anyway, read the letter.'

Eric took it from her. It was on headed notepaper, a firm of solicitors in Glasgow. It was brief and to the point.

I am instructed by my client that this correspondence is now to be regarded as closed. My client refuses to accept any further involvement in the matter in question, and to deny any responsibility for the future development of claims, should they be made, as referred to in earlier correspondence. Indeed, should any further demands be instigated my client reserves the right to institute legal proceedings for libel in regard to matters referred to. . . .

Eric frowned. 'Who was the client?'

Sharon smiled. 'Who can tell? Maybe it was something started by grandfather George. Or Flora, when she was widowed. I don't know.'

'Doesn't the date tell you anything?' Eric queried.

'Oh, this letter was certainly written just after George Chivers died, so it could well be Flora who was the aggrieved client threatening libel action, but on the other hand I would guess the issue had arisen before grandfather George died, so maybe he was the client referred to.'

'You can't libel a dead man,' Eric reminded her.

'But an action could be possible if the libel involved other people, or suggested nefarious activity on the part of others—'

'But hardly security issues.'

'Why not?' Sharon asked.

'Slim. . . .' Eric turned the letter over in his hands. 'One could always find out the identity of the client by approaching the Glasgow firm.'

'If one had the energy,' Sharon admitted. 'And provided the Glasgow lawyers didn't feel themselves bound by issues of confidentiality. Anyway, it's not all that important. I showed the letter to you just to emphasize that there have been several mysteries, a number of skeletons in the family past. What's certain is grandfather George was a somewhat secretive guy, spent a lot of time in his last years up in Scotland, fell out with his children and probably with Flora as well, could have been involved with government contracts of a security nature . . . and it all blew up into the setting up of a trust fund, for unborn children, thus finally in favour of two girls who were innocent of involvement in the quarrels, as opposed to passing the whole of his estate to his son and daughter.' She grinned at him. '*Voilà*! Why should I worry, in the end? I find myself a wealthy woman.'

'Who could have been wealthier if she had held out against her cousin.'

'Hey, what does it matter? It's only money!'

'It clearly matters to Coleen Chivers,' Eric reminded her.

'Who's running her own life, as I'm running mine. And I can't ignore the sins of the fathers – that is, the depredations of my father James Owen, in breach of the trust he was handling on our behalf.' She finished her brandy, leaned her head back on the settee and smiled at him mischievously. 'So, I'll sign these agreements you've brought for me, and then how about taking a wealthy woman to bed?'

3

Assistant Chief Constable Jim Charteris had been quite clear in the instructions he had issued. There was to be no secrecy involved in the watch to be kept on Raymond Conroy. He wanted Conroy to be fully aware that he was being kept under surveillance. It was simply a matter of increasing the pressure on the man.

'Let's be clear about this. I want you people to crawl all over him, closer than bed bugs on a mattress. When he's at home I want him to see your car parked nearby. When he walks in the street I want you to be at his back. If he goes to a bar for a drink, you'll get your elbows on the counter within a few feet. If he goes to a restaurant, you'll be ordering on a table close by. When he goes to bed and twitches a curtain he'll see you; when he gets up in the morning and looks out, you'll be there. DCI Spate will organize your rota, and you'll follow it. You'll be on Conroy's tail like dogs sniffing a bitch, and I want him to know it.'

'You told us he'd left the hotel in Gosforth where he got beaten up,' one of the detective constables called out. 'Is he on the move again yet, sir?'

Charteris glanced at Spate and then shook his head. 'No. Our latest information is that he's living in rented accommodation we've identified. Not a poverty-stricken man, our friend. DCI Spate will give you the details.'

'Could be Conroy will scream about harassment,' a detective sergeant suggested.

'Let him scream,' Charteris replied grimly. 'The whole point of this exercise is to make Conroy uncomfortable. So bloody uncomfortable that he gets out of our patch. He's walked away from the Midlands because things are too hot for him down there; I want to make sure that the heat gets too much for him up here as well. Conroy has skated away from the charges brought against him here in Newcastle, but if he thinks he can rebuild his life up here, let's change his mind. I want the pressure on, fierce. And I want him out of our area.'

It was one of the most boring assignments Charlie Spate had ever undertaken.

He organized the rotas for the seven officers assigned to the business; he made sure Elaine Start was not one of them. She showed her appreciation in bed at the end of the first week. After two weeks she repeated the performance. When he lay back finally, exhausted, bathed in sweat, he threw back the sheets from his body and told her about it. 'The guy just pays no attention to us at all. He follows the same routine, day after day. He leaves the house in the morning and drives down to the shopping centre. He buys a newspaper; he goes to a café – the same café each day – and lingers over a coffee. Sometimes he buys a second cup. By midday he's on his way to Newcastle. He parks in a side street up near St James's football ground. He takes lunch at one of the restaurants in The Gate centre. By five he's back home in his rented house.'

'Does he go out in the evenings?' Elaine asked in a tone notable for its lack of real interest. 'Does he hit the town?'

'Well, as far as we can see he has a snack at home most evenings, probably watches television, but there's been seven occasions when he's gone out to a pub. He takes three drinks: two halves of lager, followed by a brandy and soda. Then he goes home.'

'So what does our revered assistant chief constable make of the reports that are handed in?'

Charlie sighed, turned over onto his side, slipped an arm

across her naked breasts. 'He's said nothing. But he must be as bored reading them as we are in keeping tabs on this character Conroy.'

'At least there have been no more reports of the Zodiac Killer returning to his unpleasant games.'

'I think that's one of the things that Charteris has at the back of his mind. He wants Conroy off our patch. The last thing he wants is to have a killing in the area that could be laid at the door of Raymond Conroy.'

The boring routine continued for another twelve days. Meanwhile, unknown to Charlie, in the Midlands new developments had changed the picture completely.

They had been watching the clubs for weeks, undercover officers merging into the background, half-screened by strobe lights, half-deafened by pulsating, throbbing dance music. They had moved among the gyrating dancers, kept watch on the suspects they were pretty sure had been moving the drug scene on, until finally they felt they had enough evidence to crack down.

But the orders from above were to wait a little longer, until the shipment arrived.

It came in on a freighter which docked at Liverpool. The packages left the Mersey in a lorry ostensibly carrying machine tools and spare parts for the car industry. The distribution was due to take place in a deserted warehouse scheduled for demolition near the canal, and several of the pushers were in attendance. Contact was maintained by wireless between the customs officers, who had been tracking the shipment, and the local police. The operation had been rehearsed, finely scheduled, and in the event it worked like clockwork. As the packs of cocaine were unloaded from the lorry a police Land Rover smashed into the decrepit wooden doors of the warehouse. It was followed by two other vehicles: they skidded through the debris of the doors and blocked the entrance, while men in riot gear poured out of the rear doors.

Shouts rang out and the panicked dealers scurried like rats in a cellar, running in all directions but only three managed to escape the cordon, smashing their way out of one of the dirty, stained windows on the floor above, and dropping to the alleyway at the back of the warehouse.

Detective Sergeant Parsons recognized one of the men, who was running down towards the darkness of the canal towpath. His name was Dawkins: he was a skinny twenty-year-old with a history of violent crime going back over seven years. He had escaped time and again, first at the instigation of weak judges who thought he could be rehabilitated, later by pure luck, lack of evidence and pusillanimous solicitors in the Crime Prosecution Service. But this time young Dawkins was caught bang to rights. And DS Parsons had no intention of letting the young thug escape again.

In spite of the darkness he was able to follow his quarry easily enough. Parsons had been brought up in this area and knew every alleyway and narrow street on the patch. He soon guessed that Dawkins was heading for a maze of decrepit streets where he hoped to vanish, perhaps into a pub, perhaps into some dark corner where he would huddle until the pursuer lost him, gave up the chase, was exhausted by the hunt. Then he would emerge, find a safe house.

Except there would be no safe house, because DS Parsons knew the identity of the man he pursued, and if not tonight, there would be another time to take him into custody.

But DS Parsons was a stubborn and impatient man. He didn't like Dawkins. He meant to get him, and lay hands on him tonight. He was still aware of distant shouting as the rest of the gang was rounded up but he was concentrating on Dawkins. All was suddenly silent ahead of him, and Parsons slowed, stopped, listened. The streets were dark. There was a pub not more than 200 yards away where lights shone, but even they seemed muted, dimmed, as though everyone in the area was waiting with bated breath as DS Parsons stalked his prey.

At last he reached the spot where he guessed Dawkins was lying low: it was an entry between two tall, disused buildings. He thought he detected a scuffling sound and he moved forward carefully. He picked up a light creaking at the end of the entry and he flicked his torch: the beam lit up the damply dripping walls of the alleyway and the rickety door at the end wall.

It was slightly open.

DS Parsons grinned. He reached for his radio to summon assistance and then thought better of it. Dawkins was a skinny young thug; Parsons had been middleweight boxing champion in the Midlands two years ago. And he tasted his own saliva at the thought of being able to give Dawkins a good hammering.

Resisting arrest. Yes, he would enjoy that.

He walked quietly down to the doorway, opened it, and the beam of his torch flickered around and over the accumulated rubbish in the old warehouse: rusty iron, discarded boxes, forgotten, disregarded detritus. He moved slowly into the building, flashing his torch beam into dark corners.

'I know you're in here, sonny,' he called out. His voice echoed mournfully against the dark rafters. 'Come to Daddy. I won't hurt you. Not much, you young bastard.'

There was no reply, only the soft tread of his feet as he

moved deeper into the warehouse. DS Parsons moved on, watchfully. There was another scuffling sound ahead of him. 'No way out, Sunny Jim,' he growled. 'You want to get out of here, you're going to have to get past me. . . .'

Broken pallets lay against the wall to his left. The beam flickered over them, and he thought he caught the movement. He shouted and ran forward and a moment later realized he had made a mistake. A rat scampered away with a squeal but at the same moment, as Parsons was swinging around, he made out a dark blur to his right, emerging from the old boxes against one of the tall iron pillars supporting the roof. He raised an arm, the flashlight picked out the white, scared face of the man he was chasing and then DS Parsons felt a blinding pain in his forehead. It was only one blow but it sent him to his knees. His senses swam and after a moment he slid slowly to the dusty concrete of the warehouse floor.

He was vaguely aware of the echo of running feet. There was a banging sound, a door clanging, and then he felt his eyelids growing heavy as he slipped into unconsciousness.

When he finally came to, he had no idea how long he had been unconscious. He was on his back; there was a wetness about his face, a thundering in his skull. Groggily he put out a hand and groped for his flashlight, but could not find it immediately. On his hands and knees he scrabbled about on the floor until his fingers encountered the rubber casing. He stayed there for a little while, breathing hard, waiting for the thunder in his head to steady and fade and then slowly he rose to his feet, staggering slightly. He was disoriented; he flicked on the torch and was relieved to find it was still working. Head down, he moved forward, hand held out as he walked towards the door. It was only when he reached it that he realized he was walking in the wrong direction. It was an iron door. It was padlocked. He put his hand on the door, leaning, took a deep breath and stood there for a few moments, waiting for his mind to clear. Then he turned and began to make his way back towards the entrance through which Dawkins had escaped.

The bastard had got away. A sucker punch. The kind he'd avoided in the ring for years. But he'd get him. If not today, tomorrow. . . .

DS Parsons stopped, stood still. Something bothered him. For a little while he stood there thinking, waiting for something to skip back into his mind. An oddity. Something out of place.

Slowly he turned. The beam of his flashlight danced, wavered over the iron door at the end wall, moved to the padlock. A padlock in an empty warehouse. The dull gleam of oil. An empty, disused, deserted building. A newish padlock. DS Parsons walked slowly back to the door, took the padlock in his hand, felt the smear of oil.

Oil? In a warehouse that hadn't been used in years.

He stepped back, then flashed the light around until he saw the piece of timber that Dawkins had used to hit him. Beyond that he caught the dim gleam of rusted iron: it was as well Dawkins had not seen that, he thought grimly. He walked forward, picked it up, went back to the iron door.

He inserted the iron bar between the padlock and the hasp. He leaned on it, tugged. Something moved. His head was aching, there was a violent pain in his skull, but he remembered some of the ring battles he had been in, flexed his powerful shoulders, took a deep breath and heaved.

There was a grinding noise and then the hasp gave way with a scream. DS Parsons threw the lock aside and dragged open the iron door. It opened silently; no screaming, rusty protest. Oil, again. He shone his torch ahead. A wooden staircase, rickety steps. He walked forward, moving carefully downwards.

And stepped into hell.

4

The attack of influenza started at the front desk but within days it swept through the headquarters building at Ponteland. As always, Elaine Start's toughness seemed to leave her untouched by the virus; Charlie himself also seemed immune. But as the roll call of officers taking time off for recovery from the bug increased, the schedules were thrown badly out of kilter and Charlie found himself struggling to cope with the surveillance demands placed under his responsibility. It was no longer possible to have two men in a squad car following Raymond Conroy on his little jaunts. Charlie had considered asking Elaine if she could help fill in some of the difficult slots but decided against it: he had to admit she aroused a protective streak in him that he had never before recognized. And in any case, in view of the criminal acts Conroy had been charged with, keeping the man under a watchful eye was, in Charlie's view, a job for a man.

'Fascist pig!' Elaine muttered to him when he mentioned it to her.

'Who? Conroy?'

'No! You!' she smouldered at him, eyes narrowed in resentment. 'If you had your way women would be kept in the kitchen and the bedroom!'

'Hey, that's not fair,' Charlie expostulated. 'I treat you right, don't I? Is looking after you a bad thing?'

'Protecting me from big bad wolves, you mean?' she sneered.

Charlie took a deep breath and counted to ten. When he argued with Elaine he usually ended up being defeated. She was exemplary in her attitude towards him professionally; he had no cause for complaint on that score for she kept their professional relationship on an appropriate, respectful keel in view of the disparity in their rank. But privately, it could be a different matter. Particularly when they were in bed, as was the case at the moment. She was not above suggesting he was a racist, sexist, antediluvian throwback to the Middle Ages. And now, a fascist pig, simply because he had admitted he didn't really want her involved in the Conroy case.

On the other hand, he was now short of officers he could use on the surveillance. He sighed, placed a hand between her thighs, stroked her soothingly. 'All right, then, if that's the way you see things, I could use your help, with so many of the guys off sick. What about Friday night?'

She wriggled, removed his hand from her thighs, turned over on her back, stared abstractedly at the ceiling. 'Can't be done,' she asserted.

'Why not?'

'I've got a day's leave coming.'

'So take it some other time!' Exasperated, Charlie snapped, 'Hairdressing appointments aren't unbreakable, for God's sake!'

She raised her head and regarded him coldly. 'Hairdressing my arse! I'm taking a day's leave to attend a hen party. It'll be starting lunchtime on Friday, and there's no doubt we'll be getting smashed that evening somewhere in the city centre or on the Quayside or whatever. And it's no good looking at me like that! You get boozed up yourself with your mates whenever you want, and Shirley's an old friend of mine, went to school together, and there's no way I'm not taking the day off to give her proper support before she puts on the manacles.'

'Is that how you see marriage?' he demanded sourly. 'Like getting clapped in irons?'

She stared at him for a few seconds then shook her head. 'You're not going to start on that tack again, are you Charlie? You and me, we're all right as we are.' She reached out and grasped his hand, then slapped it firmly back between her thighs. 'There! You all right now?'

There seemed little point in continuing an argument thereafter.

By Friday another two men had been forced to take days off with the virus, and Charlie's schedules were struggling. He tried discussing the matter with ACC Charteris but was met with no sympathy. Charteris snarled at him. 'They're nothing but big girl's blouses, this crew! When I was on the streets there was no way officers would back off duty with a head cold! You have to carry on, Spate, with what you've got. Even if it means getting your own backside out into the cold, hey?'

Charlie scowled, kept his mouth shut, and got on with the job.

At least the routine changed little. Raymond Conroy left his rented accommodation according to his standard schedule: breakfast, lunch in the Bigg Market or The Gate, an evening visit to the Northumberland Arms, the Steam Shovel, the Prince of Wales or the Victoria and Albert. He was clearly aware of the manner in which he was being shadowed, even though unmarked police cars were used as often as not. He had probably developed a sixth sense as far as a police presence was concerned. Once or twice he had actually stopped and spoken to the officers, asked them for a light for his cigarette, obviously completely contemptuous of their dogging his footsteps. But Charlie guessed he would be edgy, nevertheless, resentful of the attention he was getting, irritated by the constant police harassment.

Charteris reiterated his words regularly. 'I want that bastard off our patch!'

The officers in the cars kept in touch with Charlie on their mobiles. He found it a wearisome task, monitoring their calls. When he hadn't heard from the patrol for a few hours he would call them; occasionally he would visit the site himself, just to check what was going on. It was what he found himself forced to do on the Friday evening.

He hadn't seen much of DS Start during the last few days. She had her own workload to deal with, enhanced as a result of the virus that had swept through the building. And she hadn't bothered telling him where she would be going for her hen party. Fridays, of course, he often ended up at her place, but that would not be the situation this week. She would take the hen party seriously as she did everything: she would be well smashed, and would be unlikely to appreciate his company. So when the patrol car hadn't called in for an hour beyond the scheduled time, exasperated, Charlie phoned the officer concerned, DC Donovan, on his mobile.

The phone rang for a considerable time before Donovan answered.

'Where the hell are you?' Charlie demanded. 'Why haven't you rung in?'

There was a spluttering sound, a sneeze. The reply was thick: Donovan clearly had a problem in speaking. 'Sorry, sir, I'm parked down at Whitley Bay, outside Club 95.'

'Changed his routine, has he?' Charlie grunted. 'Conroy inside?'

There was another spluttering sound. 'Went in an hour ago, sir. There's only me on duty so I couldn't go in to keep an eye on him. So I'm waiting in the car.' There was a short pause. 'Lot of birds gone in tonight, sir.'

That no doubt would be it. Raymond Conroy, Zodiac Killer, on the prowl. Charlie grunted, reflected on the matter. As Charteris had stated, maybe it was time he stirred himself. 'Right, just hang on there. I'll join you as soon as I can.'

Fifteen minutes later he was driving down the coast road, coming off the roundabout to Whitley Bay. Club 95 lay just off the promenade: summer evenings drunken habitués were known to stagger out of the front entrance and disport themselves on the long sands of the beach. Maybe even tonight, Charlie thought, but guessed not as the stiff sea breeze buffeted his car along the length of the promenade.

He caught sight of Donovan's car parked on a piece of wasteground near the front entrance of the nightclub. Charlie pulled his car in behind him. He switched off the lights, cut the engine, got out and walked to the driver's door. DC Donovan wound down the window. 'No sign of him coming out yet, sir.'

'Bit early for that,' Charlie grunted. He stared at the police officer seated in the car. 'You all right?'

Donovan grimaced, grey-faced, handkerchief held to his mouth. 'Not really, sir. Got the bug, I guess. Feeling rotten. I've been sick as well . . . over there behind those bins. Feel good for nothing.'

Charlie Spate was not a charitable man given to generous impulses. But as he stared at Donovan it was clear he was in no fit state to be sitting in a car late at night. He needed to be home in bed.

'Whisky,' Charlie said. 'Whisky, hot water, lemon. Bed. And a hot woman, if you can manage it. Get off home, son. You're doing no good here. I'll take over your shift, see our friend Conroy home safe and sound.'

Donovan was surprised but grateful and relieved also. He stuttered his thanks, sneezed, and a few moments later was edging out into the road, turning his vehicle towards Cullercoats as Charlie went back to his own car, hunched in his seat, swore, and resigned himself to a lengthy wait.

Just to satisfy bloody Assistant Chief Constable Charteris.

A number of women and a few men entered the club during the next hour, but no one emerged. Charlie was chilled; he rubbed the back of his neck and stared out of the window sourly. He was half minded to pack it in, and to hell with Charteris's instructions. But at that moment a small group of women came out of the club. They were drunk, as far as he could tell, shrill-voiced, giggly, falling about. They stood there in a tight group, talking loudly amongst themselves, their incoherent voices carrying down to the windswept promenade. A taxi drew up, then a second. The group had fallen to two women. Charlie saw them put their heads together, reaching some kind of agreement, and then they hugged each other, their affection causing them to lurch and stagger about on their high heels while they burst into hysterical laughter. Then they separated.

Charlie sat up and peered through the windscreen. What if Raymond Conroy came out now? A single, drunken woman going off in one direction, probably to her car; a second heading down towards the promenade. Maybe this was how Conroy selected his victims; maybe this was why he had deviated from his routine, leaving the city pubs to come out to a club in Whitley Bay. Charlie stared fixedly at the club entrance. No one emerged.

He glanced around. One of the women had disappeared. The other, lurching towards the promenade staggered, then seemed to slip, teetering on stiletto heels. She fell on her backside and waved her arms, laughing. Something cold touched Charlie's spine. The woman sitting in the gutter – he recognized her.

Detective Sergeant Elaine Start.

He sat there, stunned, for several seconds. She was drunk, incapable, smashed out of her mind, giggling in the gutter outside a nightclub. If she was found like that, if it got back to Ponteland, it would be the end of her career in the police. A career she loved. Cursing to himself, Charlie got out of his car and moved quickly across the road towards her, sitting in the gutter, waving one of her high-heeled shoes in the air. The heel was broken. It had probably caused her to stagger and fall.

She was giggling, crooning to herself.

So she sat down in the gutter
And a pig came up and lay down by her side.

Charlie reached her, got one hand under her left arm and tried to heave her to her feet. She smiled at him vaguely for a moment, then recognized him in delight. 'Charlie!' She waved her arms and continued with her singing.

So we talked about the weather
And we sang old songs together
Till a lady passing by was heard to say

'Yes, I know the old song,' Charlie snapped. 'Come on, get to your feet. We need to get you home.'

You can tell a girl who boozes by the company she chooses . . .

'And the pig got up and slowly walked away,' Charlie finished for her. 'Yes, we know all about that. Now pull yourself together. Where's your car?'

Elaine waved her heelless shoe vaguely in the direction of the promenade. 'Down there somewhere, down there. You're my pig, ain't you, Charlie? My real piggy-pig. But you wouldn't walk away from me, would you?'

She was certainly in no condition to drive. She had the next day off. She would have to come back and retrieve her car then if she had recovered from the inevitable hangover. He half led, half carried her towards his own vehicle. He opened the passenger door and bundled her into the seat. He had to lift her left leg and push it in as she dangled it outside the vehicle. He closed the door on her, put his hands on his hips, stared around at the silent street. From the promenade he could hear the crashing of sea on the rocks. There was no other person around. He had been alone in witnessing Elaine's drunken collapse. He bit his lip and stared at the entrance to the nightclub. Raymond Conroy. Still in there.

But Charlie felt he had no real choice. He hurried around to the driving seat, climbed in and started the car. He had to get Elaine home. He knew what the result would be if she was caught like this. A flow of obscenities came from his lips as he headed back into town on the coast road.

When they reached her bungalow he had to rummage through her handbag to get her keys. She had always refused to let him have a set. She was barely awake as he half-carried her indoors. She collapsed onto the bed, lying on her back, eyes wide, staring at the ceiling, and her giggles had started again. 'My little pig. . . . That's you, Charlie. And you'd never walk away from me. . . .'

He got her undressed with difficulty, pushed her under the sheets and stood looking down at her. He glanced at his watch. Raymond Conroy could still be at the club. More likely he'd have gone home by this late hour. It was pointless driving back to Whitley Bay now: he would have had to go into the club, anyway, to find out if Conroy had left or not. It had been a hell of a day; a worse evening. He heaved a sigh, shook his head, then undressed and slipped into bed beside Elaine. She was on her back, snoring. Charlie lay beside her, angry with her, angry with himself.

Finally, he drifted off to sleep.

It was a broken slumber as Elaine tossed and turned beside him. At seven in the morning he was wide awake. He swung his legs out of the bed, rose, walked through to the bathroom and showered. When he returned and started dressing, Elaine woke up. She opened one eye, watching him with a frown. Her head was probably thumping with pain. He knew the feeling.

When he was dressed, he stood beside the bed. 'I'll be going. I'd better report in. Make sure everything is all right.'

She swallowed; ran her tongue around her dry mouth. 'Charlie . . .'

'Yes?'

'You brought me home?'

'You were far gone,' he said. 'You'll have to collect your car this afternoon. Get out to Whitley Bay on the Metro – but leave it for a while. You've still got too much alcohol in your blood.'

She nodded, winced, turned over and buried her face in the pillow. She muttered something.

'What?' Charlie asked, on his way out to the bedroom door.

'I said I'm going to have to give it up,' she repeated.

'Booze?' he queried.

She turned her head to glare at him in weary contempt. 'Booze? No! Wearing stiletto heels!'

Charlie closed the door quietly behind him.

At Ponteland he checked in, went to the canteen and got himself some breakfast. He looked through the surveillance rotas and noted the name of the officer due at Conroy's rented house. He chatted with the duty sergeant, but no comment was made about Conroy and the breakdown of surveillance the previous evening. Charlie felt relieved. He went home at lunchtime: Newcastle United were playing Chelsea on television. His money was on the London side.

It wasn't until Monday lunchtime that Charlie, along with other officers involved in his team, learned the unpleasant truth.

Raymond Conroy had put in no appearance at his house, and his car was missing. They had lost track of the man they believed to be the Zodiac Killer. It was as though he had vanished into thin air.

On Charlie's watch.

CHAPTER FOUR

1

Assistant Chief Constable Jim Charteris shouldered his way into the room. His face was grim, his lips drawn in a thin line of displeasure. He sat down behind his desk then waved Charlie Spate to a seat facing him, without looking at him. There was no welcome in the gesture. He sat there for several seconds, then raised his head, staring at Charlie with hostile eyes, before he pushed a file across the desk. His tone was harsh. 'You'd better take a look at this. It came in last night, by email, from ACC Rawlins in the Midlands.'

Charlie took the file and opened it. There were several sheets inside, colour photographs that had been brightly lit by arc lamps. He looked at each of them in turn, slowly.

The first consisted of a photograph of a room. It was long and narrow; at the far end there seemed to be some kind of stonebuilt sink, while along one wall was a long narrow table. In the centre of the room was a second table, littered with implements. Charlie turned to the second photograph. It had concentrated on the stained sink, the dripping tap, the dark chips in the surface. The third photograph was of the table along the wall: it was scattered with knives, scalpels, scissors, and he could make out small, dark bottles of what were probably inks. Charlie looked up, caught Charteris's cold, lidded gaze. He turned to the next photograph in the folder.

It showed the concrete floor of the room. It was possible to make out iron rings that had been cemented into the concrete. Beside them at intervals were small metal eyelets. The floor was covered in dark stains. Charlie guessed the stains had been caused by blood.

There was another photograph of a section of the wall. Hanging from the stained wall were leather straps, heavily buckled. Charlie could guess at the purpose for their use: women had been held there, spread-eagled, arms wide, breasts straining, while the attacker who used the dungeon had concentrated on his grisly work. Charlie glanced back at the earlier photograph of the floor: there were several pieces of dirty rag lying there. They could have been used to mop up blood, or ink. He took a deep breath and looked up again at the assistant chief constable.

'Conroy?'

ACC Charteris frowned and folded his arms, his mouth twisted in distaste. 'It's a little early to be certain,' he said slowly. 'The dungeon was discovered by chance, a cellar underneath a deserted warehouse. But the officers who've visited it are pretty sure that it was the cellar used by the Zodiac Killer. They're cock-a-hoop now, because although they haven't yet received a report from the forensic labs, they're certain that there'll be more than enough DNA samples to link the murdered women with the killer. And they're pretty certain they'll soon have the evidence to fix on Raymond Conroy. Incontrovertible proof. There'll be no repeat performance, no collapse of the trial against Conroy next time. Assuming, of course, there will be a trial.'

Charlie made no reply. He could guess what was coming.

Charteris was silent for a while, his eyes fixed disdainfully on Charlie. At last, he said slowly, 'ACC Rawlins was on the phone to me this morning. He was excited, relieved, at what they had discovered. That is, until I told him that we weren't able to put our hands immediately on Raymond Conroy. I had to tell him we no longer had the bastard under surveillance. Rawlins was not pleased, I can tell you, DCI Spate. And neither am I. So what the hell happened?'

Charlie shrugged, laid down the file of photographs and spread his hands. 'Well . . .'

'From the beginning,' Charteris ground out.

Charlie hesitated, aware of the sluggish ache in his chest. 'We've had Conroy under regular watch, sir. As you ordered. The rota got a bit disturbed because of the bug that's been going around—'

'Don't give me bloody excuses! You knew the priority I put on this,' Charteris snapped. 'To hell with bugs!'

'We were thinly spread on the rota,' Charlie replied stubbornly. 'But we kept an eye on him and he knew we were watching him. It would have been better, maybe, if we could have kept a lower profile, if we could have kept our presence less obvious. . . .'

He paused as he saw the cold anger in Charteris's eyes.

'Anyway, we kept watch on him,' Charlie continued. 'Then on Friday evening last he changed his routine. Didn't go to the usual pubs he frequented. Drove out to Whitley Bay.' Charlie hesitated. 'That's why, when the report came in, I went out to Club 95 myself. I told the duty officer he could go home: he wasn't well. The bug again. So I finished the shift in his place.'

'And you saw Conroy go home?' Charteris asked.

Charlie was slow to answer. He thought back desperately

124

to the events of that night. There was no way he could tell Charteris that he had left the scene to protect DS Start. In any case, Conroy could have gone home some time after Charlie had left – but must have left again because when the surveillance had recommenced on Saturday morning Conroy's car had not been in the drive. He avoided the question.

'The next shift started at seven in the morning,' he continued hurriedly. 'The unmarked car stationed itself outside the house; Conroy's car wasn't in the drive. As you'll have seen from the report I submitted this morning, the officer stayed on watch, uncertain what to do, thinking maybe Conroy had got drunk, taken a taxi home, so he thought little of the fact that Conroy didn't emerge from the house for his usual breakfast in the town centre. After all, it was known Conroy had been at Club 95, and it was reasonable to think that the guy was taking a rest, having a lie-in after maybe drinking too much at the club.'

'Go on,' the assistant chief constable said ominously as Charlie hesitated.

Charlie pushed the folder of photographs back across the desk to Charteris. 'From that point onwards, there was some uncertainty. There was no sign of Conroy, and though a search was made around the Whitley Bay area, there was no sign of the car initially. It was finally located up near St Mary's lighthouse. Only when I got that report did I authorize the lads to approach the house. The officer knocked, checked doors and windows, but there was no sign of life.'

'And no report in to me,' the assistant chief constable remarked bitterly.

Charlie's mouth was dry. 'We weren't certain how to act. I originally thought maybe Conroy had driven home, then gone out again that morning. Finding the abandoned car threw us off track. I thought maybe we should still check his usual haunts. That's what we did most of Sunday. Then, finally—'

'You thought fit to report in.' Assistant Chief Constable Charteris seemed on the point of exploding; his mouth was hard set, colour rising in his cheeks. He took a deep breath, trying to control his temper. 'You've made a complete balls-up of this, Spate. We had Conroy in our sights – I'd issued specific orders that he was to be kept under surveillance at all times – and now, just as we seemed to have made a breakthrough with the discovery of the murder site, your incompetence has let the bastard slip through our hands. It's perfectly clear to me what's happened. Conroy went to that club. When he came out he realized there was no surveillance. That's the bloody truth, isn't it? You weren't there! The thing is, why?'

Charlie hesitated, not knowing what to say. If he explained about Elaine, both of them would be in trouble. He set his jaw. 'He went home, sir,' he lied. 'I saw him.'

Charteris couldn't dispute it, but he clearly didn't believe Charlie. 'So how come we find his car at St Mary's? He drove back there, to jump off the cliff, maybe? I wish! The fact is Conroy dumped his car, and vanished. We've no bloody idea where he's got to!' Charteris clenched his fists in frustration. 'I can tell you, Rawlins is hopping mad, Spate, and I'm in the same mood. You've put us in the situation where we've failed in our responsibilities. You, nobody else. So you'd better get things right. Within the week, Rawlins assures me, they'll have the first reports in from the forensic labs on the range of DNA found from samples taken in that hellhole. If, as they suppose, there'll be incriminating evidence relating to Raymond Conroy, you'd better be in a position where we can produce the man himself. In *custody*. You understand what I'm saying?'

Charlie understood perfectly. He had to get tabs on Conroy immediately: he had only a few days to find the man and put him in a holding cell until proceedings could start again.

That meant he had to pull out all the stops. He needed to seek help from all the people who might have had contact with the man during his stay in Newcastle.

Even the lawyers who had brought about Conroy's release from prison.

Susie Cartwright caught Eric as he was leaving the office. She wrinkled her nose in distaste. 'DCI Spate has been on the phone. He wants you to call out to see him at Ponteland: he wants to talk to you.'

'Not today,' Eric said briskly. 'Or the next couple of days for that matter. I have to get these papers signed to close down the Chivers Trust and then I'm off to catch the train to London immediately afterwards. And I expect to be there a couple of days.'

'Mr Spate made it sound like it was urgent.'

'Urgent for him, maybe, not for me,' Eric replied. 'You'll have to put him off. It'll be Friday at least before I can see him.'

Susie smiled in satisfaction. She would, Eric knew, take considerable pleasure in frustrating the detective chief inspector. She had never liked the man, and this was a petty triumph she would enjoy. 'I'll see to it at once, Mr Ward.'

Eric left the office with his briefcase tucked under his arm and walked to the car park. The drive to Chivers Properties Limited, which lay just off the A1, took only ten minutes since traffic was fairly light. There was an electronically gated car park outside the modern office building at the edge of the Town Moor: Eric spoke into the phone at the gate, giving his name and announcing his appointment with the chief executive. A few moments later the gate slid back smoothly to allow him entry.

The uniformed guard at the desk in the hallway informed him that Coleen Chivers maintained an office on the second floor, overlooking the Town Moor. He gestured towards the lift after Eric signed into the appointments book. Coleen Chivers did not keep him waiting long in the elegantly furnished, thick-carpeted reception room outside her office: the secretary made a quick call and then nodded, replaced the phone, rose and led Eric to the panelled, polished walnut door.

Coleen Chivers was standing behind her desk, arms folded across her bosom, staring out over the Moor. She turned her head as he entered, and stared at him. She remained silent for several seconds and it gave him time to observe her. She was slightly taller than her cousin Sharon, Eric calculated, dark haired, carefully coiffed. Her blue eyes were wide-spaced and challenging; and he gained the impression she would be more than competent in holding her own in a man's business world. There was a confident directness in her glance, an appraisal in her eyes as she looked at him. She was a handsome woman, somewhat sharp-featured, perhaps, but her figure was good: he guessed that in her late thirties now, she would work out regularly to keep in shape. She was dressed in an Armani suit that had probably been designed to emphasize her competence and her success. 'Mr Ward,' she said in a quiet tone. 'Please take a seat.'

She did not offer a handshake. Perhaps she felt dealing with a lawyer did not permit her to descend to such intimacies.

'You have the papers?' she asked.

Eric nodded, fished in his briefcase, and brought them out. He placed them on the desk in front of him. Coleen Chivers sauntered away from the window, picked up the papers and began to read them, wandering almost aimlessly around the room. Eric felt it was something of a performance, an actress dominating the stage of her own making. He heard the rustle as she turned over the pages but he did not look behind him: he waited quietly as she finished her reading of the documents.

'Everything seems to be in order,' she said at last, and came around behind her desk, pulled out her leather high-backed chair and sat down. She took a fountain pen from its holder. It was expensive: he caught the glint of gold. She fixed her glance upon him. 'Mr Ward . . . you have a practice down at the Quayside, I understand.'

'That's right.'

She was silent for a few moments, but the glint in her eyes when she glanced up at him from the papers was still appraising. 'Do you undertake much business in this line? Trust matters?'

Eric shook his head. 'Not really. This is being done for a friend.'

'My cousin,' Coleen Chivers commented, the smile hardening slightly at the edges. 'Yes. So what kind of work do you normally do?'

Eric shrugged. 'It's a criminal practice mainly. Small stuff. Though I also do a certain amount of work for various government departments.'

'Hmm. You were formerly married to Anne Morcomb, weren't you?' she asked casually as she finished signing the documents in the appropriate places. Without waiting for confirmation, she added, 'I've met her once or twice.

129

Business matters. Attractive. An efficient woman. And wealthy.' Her glance flicked up to Eric, in deliberate calculation. 'Anne Morcomb. And now my cousin. Is that the kind of woman that turns you on, Mr Ward? Women well-endowed financially?'

Eric found the question offensive but made no reply. He guessed none was expected. For some reason Coleen Chivers was seeking to taunt him. Perhaps test him. There was a short silence, then the chief executive of Chivers Properties Limited pushed the signed documents across to him, after extracting the few she needed to retain for her own files. 'So that's that. End of negotiations. They've been somewhat protracted. I'm pleased all is settled, at last.'

Eric gathered up the papers he would need to hand over to Sharon. 'I think you've managed to obtain what you felt was due to you, Miss Chivers.'

She was amused, smiled faintly, leaning back in her chair. 'I always fight for what I want. And I had right on my side. The depredations of Sharon Owen's father had to be accounted for. I'm pleased that my cousin also saw it that way.' She paused, eyeing Eric thoughtfully. 'So what's she like, Sharon Owen?'

Eric slipped the documents into his briefcase. 'She's a very efficient lawyer. She's making a good reputation for herself at the bar.'

Coleen Chivers nodded. 'Yes, so I hear. Maybe it's in the genes. All our family seems to have had a certain . . . drive. I've never actually met Sharon, you know. We've never been a close family. My father, and her mother, they didn't see eye to eye about much, but I suppose that's the way things go. I've heard she's quite . . . good-looking, though.'

Once more Eric felt no response was sought and he remained silent.

130

Coleen Chivers watched him for a little while as he closed his briefcase and placed it on his knees. He looked at her expectantly. He was not aware there was any further business to be concluded. Yet he was also cognizant of a certain tension in the room; when he met her glance he thought he detected a certain challenge in her eyes. She smiled. 'Do you attend many charity functions, Mr Ward?'

'Occasionally.' Rather less frequently since he had left the Northumberland landed society circuit that he'd been obliged to be involved with when married to Anne.

'I feel obliged to make an appearance at many of them, for form's sake. And for the sake of business, I suppose. There's one next week, just down the road from here,' she said softly, 'at Gosforth Park Hotel.'

Eric made no reply.

'Are you likely to be there?'

He would have described her tone as almost predatory. He shook his head. 'I'm afraid not. I've not been invited.'

'I could arrange an invitation.'

'I'm not certain I'd be free.'

'Pity.' She let the word draw out sensually. Eric rose to his feet.

'You'll excuse me then, Miss Chivers. I have a train to catch.'

She made a slight grimace, displaying an affected disappointment he was sure she could hardly feel. 'Well, if you change your mind,' she replied, rising, 'you'll just let me know. I'm sure I could arrange something. It would give us the opportunity to get to know each other a little better.'

This time, she held out her hand. He hesitated, then took it. Her handshake was warm, and hard, but when he released her grip her slim fingers glided over his wrist in a sensual manner.

In the car park Eric took a deep breath. He guessed Coleen Chivers was not the kind of woman who would give up easily if she found a man who caught her fancy. He had no intention of falling into that category.

He drove back into the city, left his car in the car park near the Quayside office and walked to the central station. Normally, when he was called to a London meeting he took a flight from the airport at Ponteland, but on this occasion he was looking forward to the opportunity to travel at a little more leisure, and work on some of the files that were calling for his presence at the Home Office.

His two assistants had been working on the latest immigration files that had been sent to the Quayside. He was fully aware that the work sent to him from London had been in part the result of his activity in relation to the Anubis affair. The senior civil servant, Linwood Forster, had bought his discretion and silence during his involvement in that affair by becoming a client of Eric's, and Eric would be the first to admit that the arrangement had certainly been to the advantage of the Quayside practice. It kept Susie happy also: more work, and a better kind of client, Eric smiled to himself.

The assistants had done a good job. Two of the files related to individuals with suspect backgrounds; they had taken up residence in Newcastle and Sunderland, and it seemed there were hints of activity with terrorist organizations in the past. The Home Office had asked for further information regarding the two immigrants, and had now called Eric to London to discuss the results. He spent the train journey boning up on the details.

He arrived at King's Cross on time, took a cab and checked into a small hotel in Kensington, then after a shower made his way to Upper Brook Street to dine at Le

Gavroche. He chose a simple Merlot with his meal, and while he lingered over it he thought back to the predatory Miss Chivers. A woman who indulged her desires, he guessed, and one used to getting her way, in personal relationships as well as business. They might be cousins, from the same family stock, but she certainly was different from Sharon Owen, even though both women displayed strong personal characteristics.

Eric was still not quite certain about the depth of his feelings towards Sharon. He respected her professionalism and enjoyed working with her; although she was considerably younger than he, they had a great deal in common, and they enjoyed a successful sex life. Though she had hinted at the possibility of a more permanent relationship, Eric was still wary of too early a commitment. Moreover, she was now a wealthy woman. And he had already been married to a wealthy woman: it brought certain problems in its wake. He was aware of his own failings: he was set in his ways, stubborn in his clinging to a small legal practice, unwilling to seek the corporate clients that his ex-wife had tried to push in his direction. It had led to conflict and it was not a situation he would wish to create again.

The following morning he took a black cab to the Home Office. The driver kept glancing in his mirror at Eric, perhaps wondering if he was someone important. He asked no questions, however. At the Home Office, after the usual security checks, Eric was escorted up the broad, sweeping staircase to Linwood Forster's office.

The senior civil servant was waiting for him. His smile was welcoming though a little distracted. It was typical of the man: he always seemed to have much on his mind, other issues of importance, riffling through possible strategies unconnected to the matter immediately before him. Charles Linwood Forster was about fifty years of age, beak-nosed and slight of build. His hooded eyes were patient, careful in their appraisals, betraying only the feeling that he had seen every foible of human nature and was beyond surprise at the indiscretions of man. He was dressed, as always, in a dark grey, pin-striped suit of elegant but slightly dated cut.

'Good to see you, Ward.' He sounded almost sincere, but not enough to demonstrate commitment.

The coffee arrived almost immediately and he settled back as Eric briefly discussed the details of the immigration appeals that he had been working on. There had been no preliminary conversation. When Eric had finished outlining the briefs, Linwood Forster nodded in quiet appreciation and suggested that later that afternoon Eric should carry on with his briefings, drawing some Home Office colleagues into the discussions. Eric returned to Linwood Forster's office after slipping out for a snack at lunchtime: the afternoon sessions proceeded satisfactorily and from the satisfied expressions around the table Eric gained the impression that his stock had risen significantly. There would be more work coming to his Quayside practice in future.

As Eric was gathering up his papers and preparing to leave, Linwood Forster detained him. 'I wonder whether you would like to join me for dinner this evening, Ward.'

Surprised, Eric accepted, and at eight that evening presented himself at Linwood Forster's club.

He gave his coat to the stiffly uniformed elderly porter at reception and was advised Linwood Forster would be waiting for him in the Gladstone Room. Still dark-suited, he nevertheless appeared to be rather more relaxed. The two men enjoyed an aperitif in the high-ceilinged lounge overlooking the Horse Guards Parade. Most of the other men in the room seemed to be cut from the same cloth as Linwood Forster: career civil servants, a scattering of politicians and businessmen, soberly dressed, speaking in hushed, controlled tones, confident, at ease, and yet curiously watchful. Forster himself seemed in an expansive mood. He gestured towards Eric with his glass of gin and tonic. 'I am happy to tell you that my colleagues were suitably impressed by the work you've put in on the immigration files we sent you.' There was a slightly mocking look in his eyes. 'I didn't explain to them how it all started, of course.'

The Anubis affair, and the price Linwood Forster was prepared to pay for Eric Ward's silence. 'I wonder what happened eventually to that statuette,' Eric said.

Linwood Forster grimaced. 'The Anubis? Who knows? Certainly, it hasn't emerged, and its importance now is much less anyway. However, if you ever do get a hint concerning its reappearance we'd like to know, of course.' He sipped his gin and tonic, paused, and eyed him reflectively. 'It was all very exciting at the time, was it not? And now I see you've got yourself involved in another fascinating piece of business. I was interested to read in the newspapers that you were asked to act in the prosecution of Raymond Conroy.'

'For the defence, yes,' Eric agreed.

'And you got him off. Do you have views about that?' There was an open curiosity in the man's tone. 'I mean, there's been a lot of public feeling bruited abroad, the thought that a killer has got away with it on a technicality. Not least because of your efforts.'

'Hardly that,' Eric insisted. 'The prosecution case was flawed.'

'Quite so, quite so.' Linwood Forster finished his drink and gestured towards the dining room. 'Shall we go in? I think you'll find the repasts provided here are among the best to be found in any of the London clubs.'

After they had ordered their meals from the extensive menu presented to them, the civil servant returned to the subject of the Conroy case. 'I read in the accounts of the trial that you had briefed Miss Owen.'

'Sharon Owen . . . yes. We put quite a bit of work her way these days. She's the youngest barrister in her chambers but she's probably also the most efficient.'

Linwood Forster nodded thoughtfully. 'Mmm. It's come to my attention that some of her opinions appear in the briefs we've sent you on the immigration appeals.'

Eric nodded. 'That's right. I've used her several times. Her opinions are well researched, and they've assisted us greatly in reaching the desired results. As was noted by your colleagues this afternoon.'

Linwood Forster poured himself a little more red wine. 'One of my favourites, this Bourgueil. Not an expensive wine, but good body. Yes, I was aware that she writes sound opinions for you. However, if I may say so, perhaps you rely a little too much upon her.'

Eric was puzzled. 'How do you mean?'

Linwood Forster toyed with his *à point* steak before he replied. 'It's merely a thought. There are other, more experienced men in her chambers that you might consider. As far as our files are concerned, of course. I mean, we would not wish to interfere in your decisions as far as other clients are concerned. No, I refer only to the Home Office briefs you are receiving and, one trusts, you will continue to receive.'

Eric knew only too well how subtly understated were

Linwood Forster's views. He sipped his glass of wine. 'I agree, there are other barristers I could use. Though I have to say I like to use the best people when I'm acting for a government department. Is there any particular reason why you suggest I should use barristers other than Sharon Owen?'

'Oh, to spread the load, of course, spread the load,' Forster asserted unconvincingly. There was a short silence while he finished the steak in front of him. 'Are you . . . friendly with Miss Owen, outside the professional relationship, Ward?'

The question meant that the civil servant already knew the answer. Eric was on his guard, surprised that Linwood Forster would have taken the trouble to look into Eric's life outside the office. 'Yes, you might say we're friends.'

'Something that would never have been acceptable in the old days, of course,' Linwood Forster mused. 'Strict separation. At one time solicitors and barristers weren't even allowed to share the same stagecoach.'

'A little before my time,' Eric said, smiling.

'Ha, of course, and even before my innings!' Linwood Forster was silent for a little while, staring at his wine glass. When he looked up at Eric, his eyes held a cold gleam in their depths. 'You know much about her family background, then?'

It was an odd question. Eric frowned and nodded. 'As a matter of fact, I've looked into her background in some depth. As part of my professional relationship with her. It happens she's one of two beneficiaries in a family trust I've been handling. Set up by her grandfather.'

'Ah, yes,' Linwood Forster murmured. 'George Chivers.'

Eric was taken aback. Then his thoughts shuttled back to comments Strudmore and Sharon herself had made about George Chivers and his mysterious activities in Scotland during the late sixties.

'The trust you've been dealing with,' Linwood Forster continued, 'has two beneficiaries, you say. Would the other person involved be Miss Owen's cousin?'

Eric nodded. 'That's right. Coleen Chivers.'

'Yes. An interesting lady,' the civil servant murmured, almost to himself. 'Do you know much about her?'

Eric shook his head. 'Not a great deal. In fact, I met her yesterday, for the first time. She's chief executive of the company her father set up, and I believe has other business interests in addition.' He hesitated. 'And, I may add, from the manner in which she's conducted the negotiations regarding the trust fund, she comes across to me as a pretty hard-headed type.' He made no mention of her predatory sexual instincts.

'Hard-headed. In matters of business, yes.'

There was an inflexion in Linwood Forster's tone that made Eric raise his head. 'Meaning?'

The civil servant pushed aside his empty plate, sipped his red wine and avoided Eric's eyes. 'Let's simply say it's fairly common knowledge in certain circles that Miss Chivers has a hard head for business, but is less . . . well controlled when it comes to matters of the heart.'

Eric sat back and stared at the civil servant. 'I'm not certain I'm following what you're trying to say,' he said, keeping his own counsel with regard to his impressions of the woman he had met.

Linwood Forster grimaced. 'I am informed that she has, over the years, formed various unsavoury, or at least, unwise connections. Rage of the loins, I believe.' He was silent for a few moments then queried, 'Do you consider the relationship between Miss Owen and Coleen Chivers to be a close one?'

Eric was surprised by the change of tack. 'Far from it. I believe they hardly know each other. They've been in dispute over trust funds, but as far as I'm aware they've never even met.'

'You're sure of that?'

'I'm merely saying what I believe to be the case, what I've been told,' Eric replied stiffly. He was getting the feeling that this dinner invitation had not really been dictated by a desire to offer the hand of friendship. Linwood Forster had an agenda: Eric should have realized the fact sooner. 'What's this all about?' he asked bluntly.

Linwood Forster sighed. 'I think you're probably right when you say the two young women in question are not . . . friends. But in the course of my long career I've always been taught that one should never go by mere appearances. Subterfuge exists, often when one becomes too relaxed to see it. I have no desire to go further into this matter, other than to say that I trust you are correct in suggesting these ladies barely know of each other's existence. A legal dispute only has drawn them into touch. On the other hand, perhaps I should also stress to you, remind you once again, that some of the issues that arise in the immigration briefs which we send to you contain, shall I say, certain delicate information?'

Eric sat very still, holding Linwood Forster's glance. 'Yes, I'm fully aware that I'm sometimes dealing with sensitive issues.'

'Which is why,' Linwood Forster said softly, 'we at the Home Office would be happy if you were to agree to use Miss Owen less often. As far as our briefs are concerned.'

Eric was puzzled. He thought the matter over for a moment. 'I still don't understand. Are you saying you regard Sharon Owen as some sort of security risk?' he demanded at last.

Linwood Forster waved a hand dismissively, as though surprised at the suggestion. 'Oh, no, certainly not, I had no intention of leaving you with that impression. But, for the time being, my suggestion would be that you should use her sparingly as far as our briefs are concerned. Perhaps if we marked certain of them in a manner that informed you we would prefer she should not have access to their contents?'

Stiffly, Eric replied, 'As my client, that would certainly be your prerogative. But I'm still curious: is Sharon seen as a security risk or not?'

Linwood Forster sighed, as though disappointed in his guest's insistence. 'No, we have no evidence of her ... Let me be frank. We cannot be sure she has no close links to Miss Chivers. They are cousins, after all. Blood and water and all that. It is better, therefore, we follow the course I suggest.'

Eric would not be put off by the civil servant's prevarication. 'I repeat ... are you saying you have suspicions regarding Coleen Chivers?'

Linwood Forster bared his teeth in a grimace. 'Ward, I really don't want to pursue this discussion. But let me say just this: Coleen Chivers is a hard businesswoman, but in her personal life she has made some unfortunate choices. It is this that gives us disquiet. Now, if you can assure me that our briefs – the ones marked, at least – will not land in the hands of Coleen Chivers' cousin, that's all I require. Alternatively, of course, if you cannot give me that assurance, we could simply send the relevant files to some other office.'

There was a short silence. Slowly, Eric said, 'That won't be necessary. I can give you the assurance. A client always has the right to ask for particular individuals to represent him.' He hesitated. 'All this ... it will have nothing to do with the trust set up by George Chivers?'

Linwood Forster seemed relieved to be released from a slightly embarrassing discussion; he almost beamed. 'The Chivers Trust? Dear me, no. We would never have had any qualms about Miss Owen's grandfather.'

Eric tried a shot in the dark. 'Is that because George Chivers used to undertake work for the government?'

Linwood Forster raised his eyebrows. 'Well, well, you do surprise me, Ward! What makes you think that?'

Eric shrugged, not put off by Linwood Forster's dismissive tone. 'I've read the trust files. There's a considerable amount of information about the family. But some mystery regarding what George Chivers was actually doing in Scotland in the sixties and seventies. And some correspondence has clearly been removed from the Chivers Trust files. I simply wondered whether it might have been as a result of secret, sensitive work George Chivers was carrying out. In addition to the businesses he was conducting in Scotland.'

Linwood Forster was smiling slightly. He was silent for a little while. Then he nodded slowly. 'Scotland. . . . Well, there's really no reason why I shouldn't tell you. It's all a rather long time ago. You're right, to some extent. George Chivers did indeed hold a commission from the government of the day to carry out certain . . . sensitive enquiries. Undercover, of course, because he had his own business activities to continue. It was in the days of the Cold War, you understand, the paranoia regarding Holy Loch infiltration, the whole Polaris business, demonstrations from left-wing groups, anti-nuclear committees, anarchists, free thinkers, woolly-scarved students and grubby tree-hugging females, anoraked subversive elements seeking to disturb our nuclear submarine arrangements with the American

141

government. All old hat, days gone by.'

'And that's why there's correspondence missing from the file?'

'I wouldn't know about that.'

'The only letter in the trust files regarding what might have gone on in Scotland draws a firm line under the business,' Eric explained. 'I have the impression it was in regard to some secret matters that George Chivers was conducting.'

Linwood Forster thought for a little while, then smiled again; it had a somewhat vulpine character. 'Oh, my dear chap, I don't think so. I don't believe you're on the right track at all. If it's in the family file, I think you'll discover it has nothing to do with the work Chivers did for us. At least, not directly.'

'What do you mean?' Eric asked, puzzled.

'*Cherchez la femme*, dear boy,' Linwood Forster replied, leaning back easily in his chair. He raised an amused eyebrow. He lifted a hand, called to the wine waiter to bring another bottle of Bourgueil, then smiled again at Eric. 'You must *cherchez la femme*.'

2

Detective Sergeant Elaine Start remained in a subdued mood during the rest of the week and Charlie gained the impression that she was avoiding him. There was no invitation issued to him to share her bed and Charlie felt bitter about it. He had stuck out his neck to save her career but it seemed to have embarrassed her. Meanwhile, his own career could be on the line after the bawling out he had received from ACC Charteris, and the deadline he had been given worried him. He was galvanized into action, of course, and that at least kept his mind to some extent off his sexual troubles.

He laid down the riot act to the officers working with him. All favours had to be called in with informants; there had to be a trawl of hotels, boarding houses and recently rented premises. Every door had to be opened to discover what had happened to the man they sought.

'I need hardly warn you of what will happen if we find a dead woman on our patch,' he asserted grimly. 'Heads will roll.'

He pored over the photographs Charteris had passed on to him: when he took in the details of the cellar, the implements, the chain-rings, he became more and more convinced the sick bastard they were seeking could be on the prowl again. He organized a check of deserted premises along the extensive waterfront of the Tyne, from Newcastle to Tynemouth, particularly where former shipyards had closed down at Wallsend, and where redevelopments had been scheduled but delayed as a result of the credit crisis. Considerable overtime was approved – Charteris pulled his own finger out over that matter – but after four days the squad had come up with nothing.

Charlie Spate had not been in the north long enough to develop an extensive range of contacts with the underworld; he regretted now that he had been forced to leave the Met, where his acquaintance with the pimps, whores, duckers and divers had been as extensive as anyone's. It could take years to build up knowledge of that kind, but he did the foot slogging necessary, taking advice from experienced officers, picking up information where he could.

It was what, finally, drew him to Eric Ward's office on the Quayside. He knew the solicitor's history: he had been a

143

copper on the Tyneside beat years ago, before he had
qualified as a lawyer and married a rich woman from
Northumberland. That marriage had given Ward an entry
into Northumberland high society but the man had not cut
himself away from the roots of his former experiences. Over
the years he had maintained a certain connection with the
underbelly of Newcastle crime, mainly in respect of his legal
practice. And Charlie knew that Ward made use from time
to time of informants along the river.

He was not happy about going to see Eric Ward. They had
a certain history, did not like each other, though they had
been forced to work hand in glove on several occasions. This
looked like being another such occasion. And the issue was
an important one. Reluctantly, DCI Charlie Spate decided he
would have to try to enlist Ward's help.

The reception he got from Ward's secretary was, as usual,
frosty, but Charlie paid little attention to that: he didn't
fancy her anyway. She was a little too old and far too bossy
for his tastes. She had a glacial look on her face when she
showed him into Ward's office, and she made no offer to
provide him with a coffee.

Eric Ward was seated behind his desk. The late afternoon
sun slanted through the window behind him, motes of dust
dancing like silver in the air. Charlie caught a glimpse of the
river, darkly ruffled behind Ward's shoulders. Ward made
no attempt to rise, or offer Charlie a seat, but Charlie pulled
a hardback chair up towards the desk, and sat down
anyway. 'I suppose you can guess why I've come,' he
grunted.

Eric Ward raised an interrogative eyebrow. He shrugged.
'I could guess, but that would be a pointless exercise,' he
replied coldly. 'It would be simpler if you just told me what
you wanted.'

'You let Raymond Conroy back on the street.'

'No. Mr Justice Abernethy did that. Because your colleagues made a balls-up of the case against him.'

'You know the bastard was guilty.'

'I know nothing of the sort,' Ward averred. 'But my feelings, or beliefs, are of no significance in the matter.'

Charlie took a deep breath. This kind of conversation would get him nowhere: it would only antagonize the solicitor facing him. 'OK, you didn't put Conroy back on the street, but you damn well assisted the process,' he snapped, still unable to contain his anger.

'And now you've lost him.' When he saw the anger rising in Charlie's eyes, he added, 'I read the newspapers.'

Charlie nodded, forcing himself to cool down. He glanced around the office.

'No,' Ward said calmly, 'I'm not hiding him here.'

'But you might have some idea where Conroy is.'

'Now what makes you think that?'

Charlie's hands were bunched into fists. He hated smart-alec lawyers. 'You acted for him. You spent time with him. You worked on his story. You got to know the man. You know what makes him tick. And my guess is you'll know why he ducked out of sight.'

Eric Ward shrugged. 'To avoid the media witch hunt, I imagine.' He hesitated. 'Look, DCI Spate, let's cut this short. I agree that after the case was thrown out I made arrangements for Conroy to avoid the press and lie low. I got him a room in a quiet hotel in Gosforth under an assumed name. But his identity surfaced quickly enough and he decided to move on.'

'He saw you about that?' Charlie asked swiftly.

'Not exactly. After that beating he took, he did hint that I might be able to help him find some other place to live, because he had decided to lie low here in the north-east rather than return to his old stamping ground in the Midlands, but I made it clear to him that my involvement with him had ended with the collapse of the case before Justice Abernethy. I had no desire to represent him further.'

'But you knew that he then found a place in rented accommodation?'

Eric Ward hesitated. 'Not directly. I'd picked up rumours that he had rented a house somewhere near Gosforth. As it happens, not far from your headquarters, I believe . . . which must have been a certain irritation. But I had no hand in that relocation. And when I got back from London on business I read that Conroy had moved on again.'

'Disappeared, you mean.'

Eric Ward stared at him calmly. 'I'd also heard it rumoured that the police were keeping Conroy under close observation.'

Charlie Spate did not want to go down that track. 'I called to see you today to find out if . . . if you can offer any assistance.' The words were sand in his mouth.

'Assistance. In finding Raymond Conroy?' There was a short silence. The solicitor picked up a pen from his desk and began to roll it between his fingers. 'I'm an officer of the court. I'm obliged to give any aid I can . . . unless the person concerned is a client.'

'Conroy is no longer your client.'

'That's true, though I am unable to let you have any information arising out of my previous relationship with him. But as to helping you finding him, I fear I can't help. I've no idea where he's gone, or even if he's still in the area.'

Charlie wet his dry lips. 'So he gave neither you, nor Miss Owen, any hints that he was about to up sticks?'

'Our relationship had ended. I don't see how I can help,

DCI Spate. Nor how Sharon Owen can assist.'

'But if you can't personally, maybe you know others who can.'

Eric Ward was silent for a little while, contemplating the pen in his fingers. He grimaced thoughtfully. 'I'm not sure what you're suggesting.'

'This is your patch, Ward,' Charlie blurted out. 'Not mine. I know I'm seen as an outsider, up from the Smoke. I had plenty of contacts down there, I know how things work. You'll have been the same up here: people you met on the beat, people you've kept in touch with, even used in your own line of work here on the Quayside. I'd like to tap into that kind of knowledge.' Charlie hesitated, watching the solicitor carefully. 'For instance, there's that character Jackie Parton. The ex-jockey.'

Eric Ward stiffened. He held Charlie's eyes. He shook his head doubtfully. 'Jackie Parton wouldn't work for you. He dislikes involvement with the police.'

'Probably got good reason to avoid us,' Charlie sneered. 'But that's not the point. I know he wouldn't work for me. But he would for you.'

'I'm not certain—'

'Listen to me, Ward. Whether you like me saying this or not, you helped put that sick bastard Conroy back on the street. Whatever you think or know about that man, I'm certain, personally, that there's a very strong probability that he really is the Zodiac Killer. Now he's free, lost to sight, wandering the north-east as far as we know.' Charlie thrust his hand into his jacket pocket, brought out several photographs, previously handed to him by ACC Charteris. 'Take a look at these.'

Eric Ward looked at them silently. He frowned. 'This is—'

'The location where three women were tortured and

murdered. Forensics are working on what's been found there: blood samples, hairs, prints . . . you name it. We're all damn sure that in a matter of days they'll come up with the matches we need. The trouble is, we'll have the proof, but we won't have Conroy.'

He realized from the glaze in Ward's eyes that the solicitor was shaken; disturbed enough to agree to Charlie's request. He handed the photographs back to Charlie. He was silent for a while, thinking, then he took a deep breath and nodded. 'I'll do what I can. And I keep in touch with you?'

'Personally,' Charlie replied, and rose to his feet.

For the rest of late afternoon, Charlie felt aimless. He drifted through the city, visiting various pubs, staying for a short period only in each of them, wandering, sipping mineral water, keeping his eyes open, expecting little but hoping for a great deal. He called in at a McDonald's, bought himself a burger and coffee, then took to the streets again. Elaine Start would be back home probably, but though he was tempted to give her a call he resisted it: he had the feeling it was best if he stayed away from her for a while, gave her time to come to terms with what had happened. They had not discussed it, but she was aware he had put his own career in jeopardy to save hers, and that the result had been the disappearance of Raymond Conroy. Somehow he got the feeling that she resented the situation they had been put into.

At 6.30 he found himself in the King's Head, down a cobbled side street off the Bigg Market. There were a few regulars there, drinking at the bar; two men were playing a desultory game of darts, and the wall-mounted television set was showing an afternoon Premier League match. Charlie moved away and found himself a seat in the corner near the door, a position from which he could keep an eye on the whole bar. He knew it would be frustrating, but at least he'd given up on the mineral water now the evening had commenced and was clutching a pint of Newcastle Brown Ale.

One of the things he approved of, at least, in the north-east.

He was halfway through the pint when two men entered the bar. He recognized one of them immediately. It was Gary Lawson, the man who had attacked Raymond Conroy in Gosforth but had escaped with a warning and the strong suggestion that he leave the north east and return to his usual stamping ground in Evesham. Charlie watched him as he went up to the bar.

His companion was looking around; he finally took a bench seat at the other end of the bar, leaning forward, elbows on the table in front of him. His face was round, yet craggy; piggy eyes were narrowed under heavy eyebrows. His skull was shaven, like Lawson's, bluish, and his mouth was sullen. He was probably about the same age as Lawson. Charlie watched him while Lawson bought the drinks. Lawson sat down, spoke briefly to his companion then leaned back, looked around the bar. It was a little while before he saw and recognized Charlie. His glance hardened; he said something to the man beside him and a few moments later both men rose, drinks in hand, and walked the length of the bar to stand in front of Charlie.

'Detective Chief Inspector Spate,' Gary Lawson said in a sneering tone.

'Mr Lawson.' Charlie flicked a casual glance towards Lawson's companion. 'Come back north with reinforcements, have you?'

'Something like that.'

'As I recall you were advised to get back south, and stay there.' Charlie said quietly.

'Did that. Till things changed.' Lawson's lips twisted in a grimace. 'But the way things have turned out I thought it would be a good idea to come back. Help you bastards do what you're supposed to do.'

'I think that was probably a mistake,' Charlie replied, his tone hardening.

'Mistake!' Lawson laughed in derision. 'You talk of mistakes! The bloody police and the lawyers let Conroy go free, and then they lose him! What the hell's been going on up here? You know the bastard is a killer, and you let him run to start killing all over again. It seems to us we can do the job you obviously can't. And that's why we're here.'

'We?'

Lawson glared at him, then glanced at his companion. 'This is my friend Nick Capaldi. You might say we have interests in common.'

The Capaldi family. Charlie stared at the man; took in the stooped, powerful shoulders, the hard eyes. He stretched his legs casually under the table, leaned back, folded his arms. His contemptuous glance swept over both men. 'The advice I gave you, Lawson, still stands. Get back to the Midlands. There's nothing you can do up here.'

'We could find that murdering bastard,' Capaldi flashed in an ugly tone, 'before he knifes anyone else.'

Charlie let his eyes dwell on the heavy-shouldered man for several seconds before he replied. 'Let me put it like this, Mr Capaldi. I know you have reason to be angry about the death of your sister – or whatever the relationship was. But don't think you can come up here and muscle your way around, in the way, I gather, your family has built a reputation in the Midlands. You're not welcome here,

150

neither you nor Lawson. Get back to where you came from.'

'Or else?' Capaldi growled menacingly.

Charlie's laugh came out as a short barking sound. 'Don't make out tough with me, son. I've seen it all, done it all, in the Met. I'm not impressed by so-called hard men. If you choose not to take my advice, that's your problem. And I mean . . . *problem*!'

There was a short silence. Lawson glared at Charlie, his mouth working bitterly. 'You let Conroy vanish. He's roaming free. Cops, lawyers, judges, you're all the same. Bloody incompetent. Well, we're not inclined to leave things up to you. We've got our own ways of finding out things; our own way of dealing with things. If you can't find Conroy, we will. And if you can't deal with him in the way he deserves, we can!'

Charlie slowly finished his pint. He rose to his feet, placed his knuckles on the table top and leaned forward, glaring at the men facing him. 'Let's get one thing clear, gentlemen. We're out looking for Conroy, but that's all we're doing. When we find him, we won't be arresting him. Unless we get information that gives us grounds for arrest.' He paused, thinking about the photographs ACC Charteris had shown him. He had no intention of mentioning it to these thugs. 'But in any case, Conroy is our responsibility. Not yours. If you're even thinking of vigilante justice, forget it. If I get one whisper that you're stepping out of line, poking your nose in where it's not wanted, doing anything to impede our activities, I'll have you bundled into the slammer before you raise a scream.'

Lawson straightened; at his side, reinforcing him, Capaldi glowered. 'You got nothing against us, Spate. We're free to stay in the Midlands or come up here. It's a free society. You can't threaten us. But I'll tell you this for nothing. We won't be idle while we're here. There's people we know up here; people who owe us favours. And we're calling in them favours. So if you're still really looking out for Conroy, better get your skates on. Because if we find him before you do. . . .'

His words died away, but the meaning was clear. Charlie slid his way from behind the table. He and Lawson were of a height; they stood glaring at each other. Charlie's tone was hard. 'I've given you good advice, Lawson . . . and you, Capaldi. Get back to the Midlands. Stay out of this business, or you'll regret it.'

'I'm shivering in my shoes!' Capaldi growled.

Charlie nodded. There was nothing more to be said. He shouldered his way past the two men, his upper arm striking Lawson, forcing the man to step aside. A small triumph for Charlie, as he saw the anger rise in the man's eyes, but little more than that.

'I just hope,' Charlie said as he made his way towards the door, 'that we won't be seeing too much of each other in the near future.'

3

That same evening, in the Bull and Bucket, located in the West End of the city, Jackie Parton shook his head doubtfully. 'I don't know, Mr Ward. It's pushing things a bit. You know I don't like using my contacts for this kind of business. Seeking out stuff for you and your clients is one thing. Working for the police is another.'

Eric understood the man's point of view. Jackie Parton was an ex-jockey who had gained a reputation, and respect, on Tyneside. He had an extensive web of contacts along the river, and Eric had used him often as a conduit for information. They had become friends, to a certain extent, though Parton continued to use Eric's surname as a mark of respect. Eric wasn't quite certain how Jackie actually made his living, but he was aware that he had a healthy desire to stay well away from the police: it helped him maintain the trust among his contacts that he had enjoyed for years.

'It's pretty simple,' Eric urged, 'and it's not really like working for the police. The fact is, Raymond Conroy has disappeared, and there's a great deal of disquiet around, after the collapse of the trial. All I'm asking you to do is to put your ear to the ground, let me know if you obtain any information about where Conroy might be living.'

'You're sure he's still on Tyneside?' Jackie Parton asked suspiciously.

Eric shrugged. 'We can't be sure. But there's no report of his surfacing anywhere else. And the last time I saw him, he told me he intended staying in the area.' He hesitated. 'If you can do this for me, Jackie, I'd deem it a personal favour.'

Jackie Parton was silent for a little while. Then, finally, he grumbled, 'This Conroy character . . . he gives crime a bad name.'

Eric smiled. 'So you'll do it?'

The ex-jockey nodded reluctantly. 'I'll find out what I can. Might come up with nothing, but I'll let you know in a couple of days.'

A couple of days put more pressure on Charlie Spate. His team were still out and about, but results were negative. As he saw the end of the week approaching he became even more touchy, and his temper was made even worse by the fact that Elaine Start was still keeping her distance. And he was aware constantly of the menacing, frustrated presence

153

of ACC Charteris in the background. Their paths had crossed once, in the reception area of headquarters. Charteris had glowered at him. 'I'm still waiting, Spate,' he had muttered in a threatening tone. 'I'm under pressure, and I'm still waiting!'

There was little that Charlie could do about it. And as the days slipped by, there was no word from Eric Ward.

The disappearance of Raymond Conroy eventually faded from the newspaper headlines. Charlie Spate's team continued with their enquiries, but it was clear they would be unable to meet the deadline set by ACC Charteris. Charlie was sweating when he was finally called in to the assistant chief constable's office. Charteris looked grim; he did not invite Charlie to sit down. In the circumstances Charlie kept himself erect, at attention.

'We've now had the preliminary reports from the forensic labs in the Midlands,' Charteris muttered coldly. 'As we've all been hoping, they've made the breakthrough we were wanting, expecting, hoping for. Trouble is, we've still been unable to lay our hands on Conroy.'

Charlie's throat was dry. 'The report . . .'

'Makes the links. There's DNA evidence from that damned cellar that ties Raymond Conroy to the killing of two of the women. Maybe even the third, but there's some doubt about that. Anyway, it's enough to haul Conroy in and start the process over again. So Rawlins is screaming at me, and as for me . . . I'm screaming at you, Spate.'

He had not raised his voice, but Charlie knew what he meant.

'So, let's be clear,' Charteris said harshly. 'This is down to you. The instructions were clear – keep Conroy under surveillance – but you failed. And I'm still not quite sure of the sequence . . . how we came to lose sight of the bastard.'

His eyes glinted as he stared at Charlie. 'Just when did Conroy slip the net? He was seen going into the club?'

'Yes, sir.'

'And leaving the club to return home?'

Charlie's hesitation was slight, but he managed the lie. 'Yes, sir.'

'But at some time in the early morning he left the house and drove away into the night. Unobserved. And unseen since.' Charteris grimaced distastefully. 'And now I hear on the grapevine that a couple of thugs from the Midlands have arrived up here to resolve our failings. Capaldi and Lawson. The last thing we want. And I hear it on the grapevine. Not from you. And you are in charge of this case, aren't you?'

Charlie took a deep breath. 'Yes, sir.'

'Not for much longer,' Charteris grunted. 'You're looking at suspension, Spate, because I'm not happy with what you've been telling me. So this is your last chance. Find Conroy. Before he can do any more damage!'

In the event, the matter was soon taken out of Charlie's hands.

Police Constable Dickens regarded himself as a history buff. In his leisure hours he watched quiz programmes on television and scoffed at the ineptitude of the contestants. He knew he could become a bit of a bore about it and tried to curb his enthusiasms when he was on patrol with colleagues, but he found it difficult. And on the Friday night of the following week, in the squad car with PC Tam Riley, he found himself cruising along Front Street in Tynemouth. It was late. The Salutation was still open for a scattering of late nighters, but the Percy Arms and the Turk's Head were closed and the street was generally deserted.

'The Turk's Head,' Dickens observed. 'Not really the head

of a Muslim, you know – it refers to a kind of knot, in fact.'

'Is that so?' his bored companion growled dismissively.

There were several cars parked along the centre of the high street and there was one parked near the monument as they crawled towards the headland, where the crumbled ruins of the tenth-century priory were outlined against the dark sky.

The car had been parked near the entrance to the castle ruins: as the squad car slowly moved forward the car headlights flickered up and the vehicle pulled away, accelerating past Percy Gardens, northwards, on the coast road towards Cullercoats and Whitley Bay.

The squad car rolled to a halt at the yawning gates of the ruins. Riley wound down the window. 'I'm dying for a fag,' he declared.

Dickens waited while his colleague lit a cigarette; he contented himself with staring out over the stark ruins of the priory. The sky beyond was a deep blue-black, and stars shuddered in the light breeze that came in from the sea beyond the headland. Fancifully, Dickens thought how a wind like this would have blown into the Tyne for thousands of years, bringing in freighters and ferries, battleships and cruisers, and in ancient times rigged timber-built ships, right back to Roman times.

'It was called Pen bal Crag in ancient times,' Dickens asserted. 'The priory was built in the tenth century. The castle was erected to protect the river mouth in about 1075. You know, Tam, the castle is interesting because it's said to hold the graves of three kings – that's why there's three crowns in the Newcastle coat of arms.'

'Jesus,' Tam Riley muttered despairingly, and cracked open the car door.

'Three kings,' Dickens continued. 'Oswyn, Osred, and

Malcolm the Third of Scotland. . . .'

PC Tam Riley got out of the car and took a long drag on his cigarette. He was unwilling to accept another history lesson. He slammed the car door behind him and strolled towards the railings overlooking the moated area in front of the castle ruins. He stood there for a little while, gazing about him vacantly, drawing smoke into his nicotine-starved lungs, then walked towards the low wall that overlooked Prince Edward Bay. The beach was understandably deserted, the tide was well out, and silver foam glinted under the pale light of the half-moon. He finished the cigarette then flicked it into the air, watched the glowing end curve down towards the beach below, then turned to head back to the car, where his colleague was waiting.

The walls of the priory and castle were to his left. As he passed the steps leading down into the grassy moat something caught his attention, a pale blotch at the foot of the steps. He stopped, stared down and realized he could make out the sprawled form of a human being. He hurried back to the car, tapped on the window, and called for PC Dickens to join him. Then he ran back to the railings above the moat.

He started to make his way down, with Dickens close behind. He flicked on his torch: the powerful beam wavered ahead of him and then steadied as he picked out the body form below him.

It was a woman. She was naked. She lay on her back, eyes staring sightlessly at the blue-black sky, arms flung wide, almost as if she had been crucified.

Tam Riley swallowed hard. He stood over the body. Behind him, he heard a gasp from Dickens as the officer saw what he had already seen. The naked torso. The dark bloodied slashes across the breasts of the dead woman. He reached for his mobile connection. Behind him he heard Dickens gasp again.

'Omigod!'

Tam Riley's radio crackled into life. Tersely, he reported what he had found, calling for backup and an ambulance. Beside him, Dickens seemed petrified. He was a young officer. Probably his first murder. He simply kept repeating himself, all thoughts of historical surroundings driven from his mind.

'Omigod! Omigod! Omigod!'

Tam Riley switched off his radio. He looked about him, the dark, stark walls of the castle above, and he thought about the car that had been driven off, up towards Cullercoats, as the squad car had made its way slowly down Front Street. It could have been the driver of that car who had thrown the body down the steps into the moat. They had possibly been only a matter of yards from apprehending the killer. Too late to even think about following the vehicle: it could be anywhere by now.

Now it was just a matter of waiting until other officers arrived.

CHAPTER FIVE

1

Eric took the late train from King's Cross that evening and did not reach his flat until the early hours of the morning. He slept badly, woke early and turned up at his office by 8.30. Inevitably, Susie Cartwright was already there: she seemed to regard it as a matter of pride to be at her desk before he arrived. As soon as he had settled in behind his desk, she tapped on the door and entered the room.

'Have you seen the *Journal* this morning, Mr Ward?'

Eric shook his head, and then took from her the proffered newspaper. The lurid headlines leapt out at him from the front page.

ZODIAC KILLER STRIKES AGAIN!
Fourth victim found on Tyneside

Eric looked up at Susie: she pulled a face at him, expressing sympathy and helplessness, and he knew what was on her mind. Many of the public would be seeking to blame the lawyers for the collapse of the Conroy trial. He folded the newspaper and settled down to read the leading article, as

159

Susie quietly went back to her room.

After three murders in the Midlands, the Zodiac Killer has struck again, this time on Tyneside. The body of a woman was discovered late last night at Tynemouth Priory. While no identification of the victim has been made public as yet, sources claim that the woman's body, which was unclothed, showed identical injuries to those suffered by the women previously killed in the Midlands.

It is also understood that the person previously charged with the killings, but released after the collapse of the trial held at Newcastle Crown Court, had stated his intention to remain on Tyneside. He now seems to have disappeared.

The question is now being asked: where is Raymond Conroy?

Eric leaned back in his chair and stared thoughtfully out of the window. After a little while he rose and went out to the reception area. Susie looked up from her desk, where she was assembling some documents into file covers. 'Yes, Mr Ward?'

'I've no doubt,' he said slowly, 'that during the next few hours there'll be more than a few calls from journalists, wanting to seek comments from me.'

'I'm afraid it's already started,' Susie murmured regretfully. 'Even this early in the morning. I've told them you're not available at the moment.'

'Right. I don't want to talk to them. Just tell them I'm busy, and have no comment to make on the matter. In the meantime, can you ring Miss Owen's chambers? I'd like to have a word with her.'

He returned to his desk and continued to stare moodily out of the window to the Quayside, until at last the phone rang. It was Sharon. He went straight to the point.

'Sharon, have you seen the newspaper this morning?'

Her tone was subdued. 'The *Journal*. I've got it in front of me right now.'

'The journalists will be hounding us very soon: in fact, they've already started on me. I'm placing myself incommunicado. You'd be well advised to do the same. I think it would be a good idea if we got together this evening.'

She was in agreement. 'Your place?'

'I'll be there by six.'

He found it difficult to concentrate for the rest of the day. His thoughts wandered; he went over the details of Raymond Conroy's defence, and the presentation made by Sharon. He told himself they had merely been doing their job, acting as representatives of the accused, making no personal judgments on whether he was guilty or not. And the collapse of the prosecution case, that had been down to Mr Justice Abernethy, who had held there was no case to answer. He wondered how the judge would be taking the news this morning. He shook his head. Like Eric and Sharon, the judge had merely done his job. His conscience would be clear.

Even so, another woman had died, and this time in the north-east. Eric frowned. If the killing had been committed by Raymond Conroy, what maniacal confidence had led him to commit such a crime again, when he was known to be in the area? The newspapers would have a field day, of course, and would be quick to point the finger, albeit carefully in view of the laws of libel. But he had no doubt that attention would also be focused on the part he and Sharon had played in the release of Raymond Conroy.

About three in the afternoon there was a light tap on the

door. Susie stepped into the room, in best mothering mood. 'I thought you might like a cup of coffee, Mr Ward.'

As she placed the cup on his desk he grimaced. 'I'll probably need something a damn sight stronger than coffee before the day is out.' He realized she was carrying another newspaper in her hand. 'What've you got there?'

'It's the early edition of the *Evening Chronicle*,' she said in a quiet tone.

'Same kind of headline?'

'Yes.' She nodded, then hesitated. 'But there's something else . . . an article inside.'

Eric groaned mentally. 'Is it worth reading?' he demanded.

Susie shrugged. 'Depends on your point of view. It's by Mr Fraser.'

Eric frowned, making no immediate connection and then, thinking back, he said, surprised, 'The guy who made an appointment with me? Wanted to talk to me about Conroy?'

'That's right, sir.' Susie placed the newspaper on the desk. 'I'll let you read it in peace.'

After she had gone, Eric reluctantly picked up the paper. The bold front-page headline read **TERROR ON TYNESIDE**. He did not bother reading the regurgitation of facts concerning the discovery of the body at Tynemouth Priory: there would be little difference from that contained in the *Journal*. He had no doubt that the nationals would be offering the same fare, and there would be similar screaming headlines in the Midlands newspapers. He opened the *Evening Chronicle* and looked inside. The article Susie had referred to was on the third page.

IS THIS THE PROFILE OF A KILLER?
By Tony Fraser

A great deal of published information has come out over the years, both in this country and in the United States, with regard to the forensic profiling of individuals convicted of heinous crimes. Serial killers such as Ted Bundy and Ed Gein in the States have been dissected, psychologically, in an attempt to discover what motivated them in their desire to rape, and torture and kill. Their mental processes have been investigated and probed, their family backgrounds pored over, their psychological strengths and weaknesses have been exposed, but while some conclusions have been drawn, conclusions of some general relevance, is it really possible to draw lessons from such investigations?

Perhaps more to the point, it might be asked whether it is sensible to apply such conclusions to the British experience. Apart from Shipman and West, we have, fortunately, not seen too many serial killers among our midst, but is the American profiling experience valid in our context? And more seriously, can we be certain that such profiling served a useful purpose in the recent decision to prosecute Raymond Conroy for the so-called Zodiac killings?

Eric read on with a growing feeling of surprise. The Fraser article went on to describe in some detail the life story of Raymond Conroy: an accountant father, the early death of his mother, a privileged education at a well-known public school and by the time he was twenty relatively well-off financially after his father's death in a car accident and a legacy from a maiden aunt. It gave some details of Conroy's work in a legal office before his decision to attempt to make a living in the art world, his attendance at an art college, his occasional sales of minor works.

Eric was thoughtful when he finally laid the newspaper

163

aside. Tony Fraser was running close to the wind. A new killing had taken place, and on the same day it had been announced Fraser's article had appeared. The article itself contained little that was not already in the public domain and was by and large an *apologia* for Raymond Conroy, with an attack upon the people who had taken the decision to prosecute him.

It was skating on thin ice, Sharon suggested, when he showed her the article shortly after she arrived at his flat that evening. 'He could well be sued for libel,' she suggested, 'particularly if Conroy takes offence.'

Eric wasn't so sure. 'I'm not sure Conroy would feel that way. Fraser is pretty careful what he writes. It's mainly supportive of the result we achieved in the hearing. It's critical of the flimsiness of the prosecution case.'

'Yes, but although it sort of claims to exonerate Conroy, the fact is it's appeared on the same day as the headlines are yelling about this new murder! It just draws even greater attention to the whole business. It's a flagrant piece of opportunism, cashing in on Conroy's notoriety.'

Eric poured her a stiff whisky, splashed some soda water into the glass and handed it to her where she sat on the settee, indignant, poring over Fraser's newspaper article. 'Don't assume too much from the coincidence of the timing,' Eric suggested. 'Fraser's article would have been written some time ago, I'd guess: it would have had to be submitted, and cleared by the editorial staff, some days before it was printed. Certainly before the killing at Tynemouth. So the timing is coincidental.'

Sharon shook her head in doubt. 'I wonder where he got all his personal details about Conroy.'

Eric grimaced, and sat down beside her, putting his arm along the back of the settee. 'A lot of it would have come from information gleaned from the trial itself, I think. Then, as I recall, there was a great deal of stuff written about Conroy's background in the newspapers, before the trial was ever moved up here to the Newcastle Crown Court. This article, it's just a scissors and paste job, Sharon. He's patched it together, using published information and larded it with a review of forensic profiling in sensational cases in the States.'

'It says at the end that there will be further articles to follow.'

'I don't think we should concern ourselves about it. Anyway, the best thing we can do is to keep our heads down, make no comments and wait to see what comes out of all this business. Remember, we're no longer involved. Our relationship with Raymond Conroy, and the murders of these unfortunate women, is over.'

She shook her head in doubt. 'We've consoled ourselves with that thought several times. I hope you're right.'

'I am. Now then, how about beef stroganoff this evening? I'm cooking.'

'And I'm paying, I suppose.' She smiled.

He kissed her lightly on the lips. 'We can talk about that a little later.'

She relaxed while he prepared the meal. After a second whisky she seemed to be at ease, and put on some music in the background while they chatted inconsequentially about the day's events, staying away from further discussion of Raymond Conroy. To the background of Rodrigo and guitar adagios he opened a bottle of Bordeaux and then, over dinner, she asked him, 'So did you have a successful few days in London?'

He hadn't quite decided what to tell her about his meeting with Linwood Forster, but when she gave him the opening he thought it best to tell her the truth. Not least because it would have a certain impact upon their future professional relationship, since he had agreed to send her fewer briefs for opinions.

'I met the guy who's responsible for putting the immigration cases my way,' he explained. 'It was OK. I mean, the Home Office is more than happy about the work we've been doing for them. But there was one thing came up in my discussion with Linwood Forster, the civil servant who is responsible for sending us the briefs.' Eric paused, delaying the moment. 'You know, when I met Coleen Chivers to get her signature on the trust documents, signing things off and closing the whole business on your behalf, she mentioned to me she'd never met you, in spite of the fact you're cousins.'

Sharon nodded, sipped her wine. 'Yes, that's right. Our parents were, as I told you, somewhat distant, the one from the other. My mother Anne never seemed interested in family reunions with her brother Peter so there were no get-togethers. As for me and Coleen later, well, there never seemed opportunity, or need, for us to meet. We didn't socialize as children, so why change the situation? But why do you ask?'

Eric hesitated. It was best to come clean. 'It sort of ties in with what was said to me at the Home Office. Linwood Forster suggested ... in fact, laid it on strongly, that he thought it would be a good idea if I passed fewer immigration briefs to you.'

Sharon raised puzzled eyebrows, staring at him in surprise. 'Why not?'

'Because you're related to Coleen Chivers.'

There was a brief, stunned silence. 'But that's absurd! What the hell has that got to do with anything?' Sharon flared, staring at him in indignation. 'I can understand if this man has problems with my professional performance, or found some fault with my legal opinions—'

'No, nothing like that,' Eric assured her.

'Because I come from the same family background as Miss Chivers? What the hell is that all about?'

Eric pushed his plate aside. He leaned over and topped up Sharon's wine glass. He could see the glint of anger in her eyes. 'It's all a bit stupid, in my view, especially since there's been no real contact between you and your cousin over the years, other than the dispute over the trust funds. But, like the typical civil servant he is, cautious to the point of folly, he's asked me to make sure that certain marked files should not be handled by you, when I need to seek an opinion.'

She was not mollified. 'I still don't see what this is all about!'

Eric sighed. 'In reality, it's not about you. It seems that Coleen Chivers, apart from being the chief executive of Chivers Properties Limited, is on the board of various other subsidiary companies, as well as being a non-executive director of some companies in which she has no financial interest.'

'So?'

Eric glanced at her. 'Have you heard any rumours about her personal life?'

Sharon grimaced. 'I don't listen to gossip.'

Eric guessed she had in fact come across rumours. 'Well, according to Linwood Forster, it seems your cousin has led a somewhat rackety sexual life over the last few years. She's never married, but there have been several relationships, varying in length and intensity. One of them has caused concern to our friend and benefactor at the Home Office.'

There was a short silence. 'You've met her,' Sharon

remarked, almost accusingly. 'So what is she like?'

Eric nodded. 'I met her in her office, to sign off the trust documents. She's a handsome woman, but she does come across somewhat . . . predatory. But that's not the point. She is what she is. But what's been of concern to Linwood Forster is the affair she's apparently been conducting of recent months with a certain George Khan.'

'Who might he be?' Sharon demanded.

Eric thought back over the conversation at Linwood Forster's club. 'According to Linwood Forster, George Khan is Iranian in origin, apparently, but became a naturalized British subject some years ago. He's currently managing director and chairman of a company called Eastern Textiles Limited. Import-export according to the classifications but . . . it seems MI5 has been interested in Mr Khan for some time.'

Sharon's eyes widened. 'In what respect? What has this Khan guy been up to?'

'Linwood Forster was discreet. Just came out with vague comments, nothing specific. But what it all amounts to, as far as I can make out, is that George Khan is suspected of having links with terrorist organizations in Afghanistan. Linwood Forster suggested there's some evidence that his company has been acting as a front for money-laundering, providing financial support for proscribed organizations, that sort of thing.'

'So why hasn't he been arrested?' Sharon demanded.

Eric shrugged. 'Who knows? Probably not enough evidence. Or maybe the authorities have been playing a waiting game. I don't know. Linwood Forster wasn't specific, and I got the impression that even he thought that there was a certain amount of over-reaction in attitudes among his colleagues. Or maybe MI5 officers are biding their time for bigger fish. I really have no idea. Linwood Forster was vague. But what it comes down to is that George Khan has been sleeping with Coleen Chivers with some regularity when she visits London. And up here, we get immigration briefs which occasionally include sensitive information. I pass most of those briefs to you for opinions to be drafted. And you're a cousin of Coleen Chivers. Like it or not, that makes nervous civil servants even more nervous.'

'But I've never even *met* her!' Sharon insisted angrily.

'As Linwood Forster said, that's as may be. But there are those in the Home Office who would see this as an unnecessary security risk. So I'm advised: make less use of you.'

Sharon frowned grumpily. 'So be it, then. I've plenty on my plate anyway. It's just that it's all so . . . irrational, as far as I'm concerned.'

'I agree with you,' Eric replied softly. 'But clients—'

'Have a right to choose who works for them,' she concluded for him. She drained her glass, reached for the bottle determinedly. She filled her glass; her hand was shaking slightly. 'Been quite a day, hasn't it?'

'Tonight will be better,' he promised her.

'I look forward to it.' She sipped her wine and took a deep breath, calming herself, and then glanced at him curiously. 'And you say Coleen Chivers came across as a bit of a man-hunter?'

Eric smiled. 'I think she's pretty direct in her attitudes.'

'So did she come on to you when you met her at her office?' Sharon asked mischievously.

Eric hesitated. 'Let's just say I got out of there as quickly as I could after she'd signed the papers. Which now make you a wealthy woman.'

'Which is the reason why you're interested in me,' she challenged.

'Well, it helps,' he mocked her. 'By the way, talking of the Chivers family, I got some more information from Linwood Forster, which helps clear up a little mystery.'

'And what may that be?'

'Hang on a moment.' Eric rose from the settee and went through to the small third bedroom he used as an office at home. He opened his briefcase, riffled through the documents it contained, extracted a sheet and returned to sit beside Sharon once again. 'You remember that letter you showed to me in the file, that seemed to have been left there after a certain amount of weeding had been done?'

Sharon frowned. 'Of course I remember it, since it was I who drew your attention to it.'

'Here it is,' Eric said, showing her the letter. 'Look at it again.'

I am instructed by my client that this correspondence is now to be regarded as closed. My client refuses to accept any further involvement in the matter in question, and to deny any responsibility for the future development of claims, should they be made, as referred to in earlier correspondence. Indeed, should any further demands be instigated my client reserves the right to institute legal proceedings for libel in regard to matters referred to. . . .

'I remember it well enough.'

'Well, when I collected these file documents from the former solicitor to the Chivers Trust, Mr Strudmore, he gossiped to me about this letter, and his view of what had happened. I didn't actually read it until you showed it to me later. Strudmore had mentioned he'd even checked local papers in Scotland and found a prison sentence was involved. I've made no further enquiry about it all because it was irrelevant to the Chivers Trust itself, but in talking to Linwood Forster at his club, he was able to fill me in with most of the details. He confirmed that your grandfather did indeed have some involvement with security matters in Scotland.'

'He was a *spook*!' Sharon laughed, put down her glass, and clapped her hands.

Eric smiled. 'Well, part-time, anyway. It now seems that part of your family fortune, as built up by grandfather George, was due to investment by the government: they put money into his firms, and in return he used his business as cover to provide them with information.'

'The dirty dog!' Sharon exclaimed. 'What kind of information?'

'Linwood Forster was prepared to talk about it because it was all so long ago, and so irrelevant these days. It was all in connection with Polaris and the siting of nuclear deterrents at Holy Loch. You know, the government's insistence on having a British, independent deterrent.'

'Which we now know was never British, never independent of the Americans, and not really a deterrent anyway.'

'And based on a nuclear submarine, located near Glasgow, of all places!' Eric nodded emphatically. 'Anyway, there was a considerable amount of resistance to the project: local demonstrations, attempts to infiltrate the base, near-rioting, that sort of thing. Your grandfather was one of those people who were instrumental in keeping an eye on things. In his case, not least by maintaining connections with a small Marxist group which included a young woman called Sally Chalmers.'

171

Sharon twisted her head to stare at Eric. 'You're not going to tell me. . . .'

Eric shrugged. 'According to Linwood Forster, Sally Chalmers and your grandfather became an item.'

'I don't believe it. He must have been fifty! And she would have been. . . .'

'Twenty-two,' Eric confirmed. 'But he was wealthy, a charming man, one would guess, lent assistance to the group in apparent sincerity, gained their confidence, and at some stage he and Miss Chalmers became lovers. Then, from the inevitable pillow talk. . . .'

'He betrayed her! The wicked old bastard!'

'He got information from her, passed it on to the appropriate quarters, and she was put on trial, along with some of her group. She served a prison term. This letter . . . well, the rest of the correspondence had been weeded out of the file, but my guess, and Strudmore's incidentally, who claims to have seen some of the letters, my guess is that Sally Chalmers at some stage later got in touch with your grandmother—'

'Flora.'

'Yes. Probably asked her for some kind of compensation, threatened to expose your grandfather . . . but Flora Chivers was a tough old lady, it would seem. She would have nothing to do with it. This letter we have here, it seems to have been the end of the business.'

Sharon read the letter again, silently. At last she asked, 'So what happened to this Sally Chalmers?'

Eric shrugged. 'Linwood Forster didn't know. She faded into the background, got on with her life I suppose. But there's the answer to the little mystery surrounding George Chivers and what he was up to in Scotland in the late sixties and seventies.'

Musing, Sharon murmured, 'You know, it's maybe not a nice thing to say, but I'm beginning to feel glad that I never knew my grandfather. Doesn't sound to me as though I'd have liked him. A *spook*, for God's sake!' She shook herself, like a dog throwing off water. 'And a betraying bastard. Don't want to think about it. Right, I'll go stack the dishes.'

'No, leave it,' Eric insisted. 'I'll see to it, after we've had a brandy. I don't want you getting too tired. We've an active night ahead of us.'

'Promises, promises. . . .'

Eric rose and poured out two brandies, returned to the settee and they sat there for a half hour, chatting inconsequentially. Finally, when the drinks were finished he went out to the kitchen and stacked the dishwasher. He was becoming quite domesticated, he thought wryly. From the other room he heard voices and music: Sharon had switched on the television.

He finished stacking, ran his hands under the tap, picked up a towel and wandered back to the sitting room. Sharon was standing in front of the television set. She reached down and switched it off. When she turned to face him her eyes were wide, her features pale.

'What's the matter?' Eric asked, concerned.

She half turned her head, gesturing towards the television set. 'The first item . . . it was about the woman murdered at Tynemouth. They say the body has been identified.'

Eric walked forward and took her in his arms. 'So what's the problem?'

She was shaking. 'The body . . . the dead woman. . . .' She raised her shocked face to his. 'It's been identified as my cousin.'

'What?' Eric said, astonished.

'That's right. Coleen Chivers.'

173

2

The briefing room was packed: additional officers had been drafted in to expand DCI Spate's team, now that the issues had changed with the receipt of forensic information from the Midlands. The surveillance of Raymond Conroy, and the loss of contact with him, had now metamorphosed into the hunt for a murderer.

Normally on such occasions there would have been a buzz of anticipation, a chattering, murmuring, discussions going on all around the room, but this was different: the room was virtually silent, even down to the rustling of paper. It was as though all the officers in the room were waiting for something dire to occur, holding their breaths for the next bit of bad news. Assistant Chief Constable Jim Charteris was not present, but Charlie Spate was keenly aware of his brooding presence outside the room. He'd be ensconced in his office, but Charlie knew what the man would have on his mind.

Charlie looked down at the file in his hands. A similar file had been passed to each officer in the room. It contained photographs of the dead woman, the crime scene, some close-ups of the marks on the corpse, a list of names with brief notes attached.

'Right. Listen up.'

Charlie looked around the assembled officers and caught Elaine Start's glance. Her mouth was twisted in distaste: he knew she was offended by his use of the Americanism. His eyes slipped away from her, challenging others in the room.

'Let's take a look at these photographs first,' he announced. 'Some of them cover the work undertaken by officers in the Midlands. They relate to the killings of three women, the Zodiac killings, and there's a few shots of the location – now confirmed by forensics – where they died. The details have not yet been made public knowledge, because the results came in only this morning, but the location, this cellar shown in the photographs, is now positively linked to Raymond Conroy by DNA evidence. We're now certain – not that we ever doubted it much – that Conroy really is the Zodiac Killer. These photographs are for your information and background only. In themselves they give us a reason for looking for Raymond Conroy, but as far as we're concerned we need to focus on what's happened up here on our patch. The murder of Coleen Chivers. You'll all probably know the location where Dickens and Riley found the body. Tynemouth Priory. A car was seen driving away from the location minutes before the body was discovered. No description available, but we can surmise it may well have contained the killer. The arrival of the squad car may well have disturbed Conroy so he was unable to complete his work.'

He held up one of the photographs and waved it. 'Pay particular attention to this shot of the woman's breasts. Note the marks across the flesh, a sharp instrument, maybe a knife, more likely a scalpel. Forensic will confirm in more detail later. But check them out against the marks shown on the other dead women. The marks tell us who we'll be looking for. The guy the newspapers have labelled the Zodiac Killer.'

He paused, letting his glance travel around the silent officers. 'We all know what that means. Ever since the collapse of the hearing after which Raymond Conroy was released we've had the man under surveillance, until he slipped out of sight. We are now aware that there is confirmation from forensic evidence that Conroy was indeed involved in the murder of the three women in the

Midlands, in spite of what Mr Justice Abernethy might have concluded after the lawyers had got their teeth into the existing evidence at the time. But now this has happened: the murder of Coleen Chivers. So you know what I'm about to say: it's absolutely essential that we trace Raymond Conroy, whom we believe has gone to ground somewhere up here in the north-east, essential we find him, bring him in for questioning. The case against him over the Midlands murders has collapsed, of course, but we need to talk to him again now, and urgently. Not for what he did in the Midlands, but for what he's probably done up here.'

He almost added it was a matter of pride, but refrained from doing so. The room remained silent. He had expected that someone would have raised some doubt, querying whether they were correct in merely assuming the Tynemouth Priory killing had been done by Conroy, irrespective of what had occurred in the Midlands, but no one spoke, though he observed that there was a frown on DS Elaine Start's brow as she stared at the photograph referred to.

'So that's the first task, and our number one priority: find Conroy. But that doesn't mean we neglect other lines of enquiry. We've had information passed to us from London – for once the bastards down there seem to have paid attention to what goes on in the north.' His comment raised a faint smile on some faces: he was known to be a southerner himself previously from the Met, and they knew that this was a way of trying to bond the group to his objectives. He grunted, then selected a different photograph. 'This is a photograph of one George Khan. Good-looking bastard, isn't he? It seems the dead woman was a bit of a randy piece, chief executive of a big company, and that this character was the latest in a line of lovers. Enquiries are currently being

176

made in London as to his whereabouts at the moment: it seems he's not been seen at his office or home for some days. There's a view that he might well be up here, though we can't be certain of that. Anyway, keep your eyes skinned. We can't ignore the possibility that this killing was motivated by a lovers' quarrel. So, Meredith, Jones and Sampson, you'll be checking through the list of men she'd been involved with. Usual stuff. Not least, the last time they might have seen her, nature of their relationship with her, alibis for the night in question. Charlton, you'll be responsible for liaison with the Met and their contact with the Home Office.'

Charlie took a deep breath. 'Right. That brings us to one other thing. We may be hunting Raymond Conroy but he had his enemies. Two of them are known to us. I've met them myself, a few days ago, here in the north-east. One is Gary Lawson; another is Nick Capaldi. They're both based in the Midlands but they're up here, and they think of themselves as hard lads. I don't want them getting in the way of our enquiries. So you, Salmond, will co-ordinate a search for these two guys, along with DC McManus. I want them hauled in, questioned, and if there's nothing to be got out of them, I want their arses kicked back to the Midlands, out of our way.'

He closed the file, stuck it under his arm and surveyed the room silently for a few moments. 'Now we don't know quite how Coleen Chivers fell into the killer's hands. We have information that she was at a charity dinner in Gosforth earlier that evening, but left early. She was seen in a bar close by to the Gosforth Park Hotel, probably in the company of a man, but we have no clear description of this person. Maybe we should assume it was Raymond Conroy, but let's not get carried away. Could have been Khan. We have no identifiable time for her leaving the bar, and there's been no sighting of her after that event. Her car was discovered nearby: forensic are still combing through it. My guess is we'll not get much from it. The killer probably took her away in his own car though how the hell he enticed her into it, God only knows. But when she was found, she'd been stripped, so we need to find any items of her clothing that may have been discarded in the area. We also have no information just yet as to the time of death. Dickens and Riley can confirm that it looks as though she was strangled, slashed and then dumped. But all this means you've got plenty of lines of enquiry to follow. You'll see from the sheets in front of you the make-up of the teams, who's leading the groups, and where your priorities lie.'

He put his head back, challengingly. 'And let's get one thing clear. We're certainly not going to be working in a bubble here. The press are going to be on our necks; the public will be harassing us. I need hardly tell you, so will the top brass. This is urgent, guys. So keep your mouths shut while you follow your enquiries. But first things first. Find Raymond Conroy!'

The groups began to break up, some leaving the room, some staying where they were, studying the file. Elaine Start remained where she was, reading the reports from the forensic labs in the Midlands, studying the photographs. Charlie returned to his office.

Some twenty minutes later there was a light tap on the door and Elaine Start looked in on him. 'Can you spare me a few minutes, sir?'

Charlie leaned back in his chair and beckoned to her to come in. She closed the door behind her, quietly. There was a slight frown on her face and she seemed a little edgy.

'So how can I help you, DS Start?' he said in a formal tone.

There was a hint of mockery in his voice as he adopted the

same formality she did when they were in the office together. Whatever happened between them when they were between her sheets was not referred to here. She straightened, opening the file he had given her. 'It's about some of the details noted here, sir.'

'What about them?'

'Well, the first thing is, the cuts on Coleen Chivers' breasts. They're somewhat . . . crude.'

'How do you mean?'

Elaine placed several photographs on the desk in front of him. 'These are the shots taken of the victims of the Zodiac Killer. We all know, because the papers have been screaming about it from the beginning, that the killer seems to have so-called artistic leanings. He got his kicks by keeping the women alive, it seems, in that cellar we now know about, while he used a scalpel to torture them, carving Zodiac signs on their bodies, inking the marks later to outline the sign. I have to admit I don't see much artistry in them, just a series of cuts linking specific points. . . .'

'I don't suppose he was able to draw the full figures of Sagittarius and Libra in detail,' Charlie replied a little irritably, 'with the victims presumably struggling and yelling. But I get the picture, if you'll excuse the pun.'

Elaine clearly thought the remark flippant. 'That's not really the point I want to make,' she said. 'The fact is, if you look at the cuts made on the women in the Midlands they're clearly defined, precise in their lines. That's not the case with Coleen Chivers. It's not even possible to see what design the killer had in mind. To me they just look like . . . cuts.'

Charlie sighed. 'I don't think you can have been listening closely enough to my briefing. A car was seen leaving Tynemouth Priory. Conroy had taken the woman there, naked, strangled her, cut her about—'

'But previously he'd done that in a secure hideout!'

'Damn it, he's not been up here long enough to find a safe house!' Charlie snapped, losing patience unreasonably. 'Can't you see that? Look, my view is that the urge was on the perverted bastard again, he wanted to satisfy it, he grabbed the Chivers woman, strangled her, carved her ... but couldn't do his normal fastidious job on her as he did the others because he didn't have an available cellar and time. And he was probably disturbed when the police car turned up in Front Street.' He glared at her. 'You don't seem convinced.'

She was silent for a little while. Then she took a sheet from the file and stared at it. 'This report from the Gosforth lab—'

'They've not had time to produce a full report,' Charlie interrupted dismissively. 'It's just a few findings, preliminary stuff.'

'But it states that there were traces of the date-rape drug, rohypnol, in the body. There's no evidence in the other three cases, in the Midlands, of the use of such drugs.'

Charlie sighed theatrically. 'Detective Sergeant Start, let's compare like with like before we jump at issues like that. The killing of Coleen Chivers naturally differs from the cases in the Midlands. It wasn't planned as carefully. There was no safe house where Conroy could hide the woman while he tortured her. And because of the periods during which he held his previous victims, there's no way we can know whether or not he used rohypnol or any other drug at any particular time in the killings. So just exactly what are you trying to say? What's bothering you?'

Elaine Start raised her head and held his glance stubbornly. 'I just don't think we should jump to conclusions without looking at all the evidence.'

'You think Raymond Conroy didn't strangle the Chivers woman?' Charlie demanded.

She hesitated. 'I didn't say that. I—'

'You don't think we should treat Conroy as our major suspect?'

'I'm not sure. I mean, this Khan guy—'

'You don't think we should look for Conroy as a main priority?' Charlie insisted savagely.

Elaine Start's mouth was set firm. She made no reply.

Charlie Spate regarded her coldly for a little while. Then he nodded. 'OK, so you've made your point. I've heard you out. But I'm sure we both agree I'm in charge of this investigation. And I'm sure you agree it's worrying that Raymond Conroy, a suspected killer, should have disappeared from our screens. And I'm also certain, now, that you'll follow instructions and give every priority to hunting that perverted bastard. Others are checking on Khan. And when we find Conroy, well, I guess we'll be able to get answers to all the questions you raise, won't we?'

His eyes reflected his displeasure. Elaine stood rigidly in front of his desk, almost at attention. Then, quietly, she picked up the photographs, slipped them back into the file and turned towards the door. When she reached it, she hesitated. She looked back at him. Her tone was reluctant, suddenly uncertain. 'There's one more thing. I . . . I haven't got around to, well, thanking you.'

Charlie raised his eyebrows but made no reply.

She was unable to meet his eye. 'Last week, when you rescued me from Club 95. If I'd been picked up in that state, it could have cost me my career.'

'Probably,' he replied coldly.

She took a deep breath, her magnificent bosom rising. For

181

once he was not distracted. 'And if you hadn't taken me home,' she added, 'you wouldn't have lost track of Conroy.'

'That's true.'

He wasn't making it easy for her. She raised her eyes, staring at him sheepishly. It was an odd situation, a new development in their relationship. Although he was the senior officer, it was Elaine who always seemed to be in control in their personal lives. For once, she was caught awkwardly, unable to retain her composure. She ran a hand nervously over her mouth. 'Well, I just feel I ought to say thanks, and sort of apologize to you. For putting you in that position, I mean. And thank you, for not spilling the beans to ACC Charteris.'

Charlie shrugged dismissively. 'I could hardly do that, without exposing my own behaviour.'

'Yes, but . . .' Her voice died away. Her glance flickered around the room, then returned to hold his. 'Anyway, I've been slow in telling you I appreciate it. I needed to think things over, you see, and that meant I couldn't say anything straightaway.'

'Let's forget it,' Charlie said airily, and busied himself with the papers in front of him. After a short silence he looked up, to see Elaine still standing in the doorway.

'I was wondering . . . will you be coming around on Friday night?' she asked.

Charlie's eyes narrowed. Then he shook his head. 'No, I don't think that would be a good idea.'

It was as though he had struck her. She stiffened, held his glance for a few seconds then opened the door and left the room. The door closed behind her. The soft click of the lock had the sound of cold finality.

3

Inevitably, the newspapers retained the story in front-page headlines for the next few days, and there was considerable coverage on the regional television programmes. By the end of the week criticism of the police became more vocal: the fact of the botched police surveillance was leaked to the press and the question was asked, how could they have allowed a suspected murderer to vanish without trace? Eric discussed it with Sharon Owen when they met for dinner in the city.

'They're being careful not to mention Conroy by name,' she said.

'Even though it's obvious it's him they're referring to,' Eric agreed.

They had both read the potted history of the life of Coleen Chivers churned out in various newspaper articles. There was extended coverage of her business successes, her activities in various projects, and some guarded comment on her social life.

'They're skating around her personal life a bit,' Eric mused, 'but there's enough to be read between the lines to suggest they know about her somewhat rackety indiscretions.'

Sharon shook her head. 'At least no one yet seems to have picked up the family connection with me. Let's hope it stays that way.'

It did not, of course. Early the following week, the news broke in the *Journal*. An investigative reporter had traced the family tree, first back to the link with the Chivers Trust and their grandfather George Chivers, and then to Sharon's mother, and her brother Peter, who had sired Coleen Chivers. There was even a mention of the scandalous behaviour of Sharon's father, the solicitor James Owen, who had depleted the funds available to the beneficiaries of the Chivers Trust. Eric wondered whether the leak would have been the result of questions asked of the former trust solicitor, Strudmore. There was a certain gossipy quality about Strudmore's confidences, and he was the most likely source.

Sharon took it fairly philosophically. They met for a coffee at the Malmaison on the Quayside, close to Eric's office and her chambers. 'It was inevitable they'd fish out the information,' she said gloomily. 'But there's nothing I can do about it. There have been a few phone calls from journalists. Not very welcome, but I've been polite. And dismissive. I didn't know Coleen Chivers. I had never met her. I have no comments to make on the manner of her death. And I've refused to discuss the fact that I had defended Raymond Conroy.' She hesitated. 'Or as one journalist put it, the man who has since murdered my cousin.'

'That's yet to be proved,' Eric muttered.

'I put the phone down on the guy when he said that.' Sharon toyed with her coffee spoon, staring out of the window down towards Wesley Square, and across the elegant curving arch of the Millennium Bridge towards the Baltic Centre. 'But what do you think, Eric? Did Conroy do it? Did we help get him off the Midlands murder charges, only for him to kill again?'

'We did our job, Sharon. That's all. And it's not yet been proved that Conroy did kill Coleen Chivers. It's not something that deserves our attention.' Even as he said it his mind slipped back to the interview with DCI Charlie Spate, when he had asked Eric for his assistance in using Jackie Parton as an informant. He hadn't mentioned it to Sharon, and he saw no reason to do so now. He had heard nothing from the ex-jockey, but he was sure that if Jackie Parton came up with any information he would hear of it before any report was made to DCI Spate.

'Have you had a visit from the police?' Eric asked curiously.

Sharon frowned. 'Just a brief one. After the article came out, actually. They just wanted to ask me about the Chivers Trust. Sort of hinting that maybe I could have profited from the death of my cousin, as far as trust monies were concerned. I put them straight on that one. Since the agreements were signed, and witnessed by you, my rights to the funds are circumscribed. It's her estate that'll get what she was due under the Chivers Trust; nothing to do with me. And I can hardly believe she'd have mentioned me in her will. If she'd even made one. The officers ... they seemed satisfied by that. And I've no doubt they've already checked that I was not in her social circle.'

Eric nodded. 'I see that Tony Fraser has continued with his series on Raymond Conroy.' He shook his head, puzzled. 'I'm surprised the editors are still happy to take the pieces. I mean, with this new killing, and Conroy on the run, they're taking a chance ... though their own lawyers will have vetted the writing for possible libel.'

'Yes, I saw what Fraser had written. There's a hint of further startling revelations,' Sharon mused, 'but that's probably journalistic licence to keep up interest. As far as I can see Fraser has just about run out of information he could have obtained from what's already been written about Conroy, or came out during the hearings in the Midlands and up here at Newcastle Crown Court.' She finished her coffee, replacing the cup firmly. 'Anyway, that's it. I'd better get back to my chambers. I've got a stack of opinions to write.' She glanced at him quizzically as she rose. 'But not on recent immigration matters.'

Eric laughed. 'I'm afraid they've dried up as far as I'm concerned too. Either Linwood Forster is being very careful, or the Home Office has sorted out all its concerns about illegal immigrants.'

'I can hardly believe that.' She stood beside the table, looking down at him. 'Of course, with Coleen's death, the problem about security of the files has sort of gone away, hasn't it? So there's no reason why you shouldn't use me for opinions in the future.'

'Rest assured, my love, I don't imagine anyone will look upon that as a possible motive for murder. You're in the clear.'

She grinned at him. 'Who knows what lies in the mind of a woman?'

As the days passed the furore died down somewhat in the newspapers, being succeeded by accounts of a wreck in heavy seas off the north-east coast, a case of smuggling cigarettes in Hartlepool, and the confiscation of a haul of heroin in Yarm, the result of a Customs and Excise investigation that had been carried out over the previous three years. Eric recognized the names of two former clients of his firm. Fortunately, he had not been asked to defend them.

While he was on his way back from a magistrates hearing at Berwick-upon-Tweed, he decided to make a diversion to visit his ex-wife Anne at Sedleigh Hall. She invited him to dinner, and offered him a bed for the night. Naturally, she asked for his views on the murder of Coleen Chivers, wondering whether it really had been the work of the man he had earlier defended. He shrugged the questions aside. There was already too much theorising in the media.

'Anyway, I'm glad you're here, Eric,' she said, 'because I've been meaning to ask you to take a look at some of the contracts I've been asked to sign. Not tonight, but if you've time before you leave for Newcastle in the morning, perhaps you'd be kind enough to cast an eye over them. For an appropriate fee, of course,' she added, smiling.

'What do they concern?'

Anne explained that the growing recession had caused a number of European-funded projects that she was overseeing to be placed in jeopardy. Unbeknownst to Eric, she had been devoting more time of late to the oversight and supervision of contracts with suppliers in the north-east, likely recipients of money from the European Social Fund.

'No longer a hard-headed businesswoman, but a philanthropist!' he exclaimed. 'So you after a life peerage or something?'

'And sit with all those old fogies in the House of Lords?' she scoffed. 'Hardly that! But I've got most of my business activities under control now, I've good managers and administrators in place and . . . well, the gap you left, I've managed to plug.'

'Except in this instance,' Eric suggested.

'I suppose so. But you do come cheaper than some of the firms of lawyers I deal with!' she laughed.

The following morning Eric spent rather longer than he had expected in discussing the contracts with Anne. Some of them raised issues which she had not contemplated and together they discussed the implications and the pitfalls which might arise in the future were she to conclude the agreements. She invited him to stay for lunch and he took the opportunity to spend an hour walking around the estate in the late morning sunshine. It brought back memories of the time they had spent there together, and a degree of nostalgia touched him. But they were days long past, and both he and Anne knew they had moved on of recent years: there was no reliving of the relationship they had enjoyed.

When he returned from his walk among the ancient oak trees that lined the avenue leading down to the meadows, Anne met him in the hallway, at the foot of the grand staircase. 'There was a call from your office while you were out.'

'They rang here?' Eric fumbled in his pocket for his mobile, then muttered a curse. He had left it in the office.

Anne smiled. 'You can return the call in the library. Susie implied it was sort of urgent.'

Eric walked through to the library, sat down at the long mahogany table and picked up the phone. Susie answered it almost immediately. 'Mr Ward! I've been trying to get hold of you. I expected you back in the office this morning.'

'I've been detained here. So what's the problem?'

There was a slight hesitation. 'I've been asked to make sure you call this number.' She read it out to him, then paused again. 'It's Raymond Conroy.'

Eric frowned. A brief image of all the newspaper headlines flashed across his mind. 'What the hell does he want to speak to me for? I don't act for him any more.'

'He didn't give any explanation,' Susie replied primly. 'But he seemed more than a bit flustered, sort of agitated.'

Eric hesitated, then nodded. 'As I would be in his situation. All right. Give me the number again.'

He took a pen from his pocket and wrote down the mobile number Susie gave him. After he'd replaced the phone he thought for a few moments, then punched in the number for Sharon Owen's chambers. The clerk informed him she was not there. Eric tried her mobile. It was switched off.

Finally, he rang the number Susie Cartwright had given

him. The phone rang out for a long time before it was answered.

'Ward?' The voice was strained, and the man was breathing hard, as though he had been running. There was a muffled quality to the voice also, a thickness that caused a distortion in his tones. 'Ward? This is Conroy.'

'You wanted me to call you.'

'I have to see you. It's urgent.'

'What about?' Eric asked carefully.

'Can't you guess? But I can't discuss it over the phone. I need to see you. Come to me and—'

'Conroy,' Eric interrupted, 'I don't think this is a good idea. I'm no longer your legal representative. No doubt you're fully aware the police have been searching for you. You'll have seen the newspapers. I give you this bit of advice freely. You need to contact the police, hand yourself in and—'

'It's all rubbish! It's crazy! The stories in the newspapers, they're all lies! The police are trying to frame me again, the way they did over the killings in the Midlands! I need to see you, Ward, to sort this out. There are things I didn't tell you when you were acting for me. I need to talk to you. It's urgent, goddamn it! I've got to talk to you!'

The words came out in a rush. The man was almost babbling, and it seemed to have affected his voice. It was almost as if Eric was talking to a stranger, and he was unable to discard the impression that the speaker was at the end of his tether.

'I still think you should see the police. If you can explain to them—'

'No! I'll explain to you. Ward, you must come to meet me. I'll explain everything then. I don't want to talk to those other bastards. They've already tried to railroad me once. I don't trust them!'

189

There was a short silence. Eric sighed. 'All right,' he said reluctantly. 'I'll come to meet you. Where are you at the moment?'

'I'll be waiting for you. Rowland's Farm. It's in the Coquet Valley, not far from Warkworth.'

Eric knew the area. He glanced at his watch. 'If you can give me more precise directions, I should think I'll be there in about an hour or so.'

Susie Cartwright liked Jackie Parton. She could not say precisely why the sight of him always cheered her up: perhaps it was his cockiness, his jaunty, rolling walk, his ready smile. Or maybe it was because he flattered her, paid her attention, made her feel good. So when he walked into the office she smiled at him. There was no need for him to make an appointment if he wanted to see her employer. DCI Spate she would always be difficult with: Jackie Parton she would accommodate. She would always see to that.

'You're out of luck today,' she announced. 'He's not in.'

Jackie Parton seemed unusually subdued, and there was a frown on his narrow features. 'What time do you expect him to get back?'

She shrugged. 'He should have been in this morning, but I finally traced him to Sedleigh Hall. He'd called in to see Mrs Ward.' She still could not bring herself to use Anne's maiden name. She still remained concerned that things had come to such a pass that they had divorced. 'I expect him back later this afternoon.'

'I've tried his mobile.'

'He left it in the office yesterday. He's often forgetful that way,' she muttered, sighing and shaking her head. 'He can be so old-fashioned, you know. I keep telling him he ought to accept modern technology less reluctantly. But he still leaves the phone behind from time to time.'

Jackie Parton hesitated, then walked around the room a couple of times, as though weighing up something in his mind. At last he nodded. 'OK, when he comes in, or if he phones you before he reaches the office tell him I've been in. Tell him. . . .' Jackie Parton hesitated. 'Tell him I need to talk to him because I know where Raymond Conroy is hiding out, and I need to—'

'Mr Conroy?' Susie's eyes were round. 'He's already been in touch.'

'What do you mean?' Jackie asked huskily.

'Mr Conroy rang here, wanted to speak to Mr Ward urgently. I finally traced Mr Ward to Sedleigh Hall and passed on the message.'

'What did Conroy want?' Jackie Parton asked urgently.

'I don't know.' Susie seemed a little flustered by the stridency in the ex-jockey's tones. 'I just passed on the message that Conroy wanted to speak to him. I presume Mr Ward will have rung him back. Is there anything I need to know? Or do?'

Jackie Parton bared his teeth in a grimace, thinking about it for a few moments. 'I think . . . I think you'd better place a call to DCI Spate, and tell him. . .' The words died away, the instruction unfinished. Susie understood: she was aware that the ex-jockey disliked dealing with the police. He shook his head. 'No . . . no, never mind. Forget it.'

He turned away briskly, heading for the door.

'Are you sure?' Susie asked nervously.

'No. It's all right. I'll see to things myself.'

CHAPTER SIX

1

Eric drove deep into the higher reaches of the Upper Coquet Valley in a reflective mood. He could not escape the niggling, persistent feeling at the back of his mind that in following Conroy's instructions he was doing the wrong thing. He had represented the man at his trial, engaged Sharon as counsel, and together they had successfully exposed the weakness of the prosecution case. But neither he nor Sharon had obtained a deal of satisfaction from the outcome: Raymond Conroy had come across to them as arrogant, sneering and contemptuous. And what was worse, Eric had all along suspected that they had been acting for a cold-hearted killer.

Now, of course, with the whole of the north-east hunting Conroy, the situation was even more sensitive. Coleen Chivers had been strangled and scarred in a manner similar to the women in the Midlands. So what the hell was Eric doing driving to meet the man?

Curiosity.

He could put it down only to curiosity. Over the phone Conroy had suggested he had revelations to make, things he had not disclosed to his solicitor and barrister previously, and perhaps it was this that had finally drawn Eric to agree to meet the man again. But in addition, Eric needed to assuage the essential guilt that had troubled him ever since the acquittal of Raymond Conroy: the possibility that he had had a hand in effecting the release of a homicidal maniac. The guilt, thrust aside and largely unacknowledged, was there constantly at the back of his mind: possibly it had been the reason why he had walked away from Conroy immediately after the aborted trial. In going to meet the man now, talk to him, hear what he had to say and perhaps persuade him to give himself up to the police, Eric would perhaps be able to clear his conscience.

He wished he could have been able to speak to Sharon. She was a clear-headed woman. She had been as deeply involved with the release of Raymond Conroy as he; she might have dissuaded him from taking this step. She may well have persuaded him to simply contact the police. Now, he was committed. It was still possible to turn back, of course, but as he crossed the warm, sun-dappled hills and dropped down to the curling, glinting river he knew he had come too far to back away.

He had left the ancient town of Warkworth with its historic castle and twelfth-century bridge behind him. He followed the swinging meander of the river and caught a glimpse of a solitary, unmoved heron on the riverbank before he turned off as directed by Conroy onto a side road, a broad rutted track that began to climb up to the steep side of the fell, giving glimpses of the Cheviot hills on the skyline. A young fox crossed the track in front of him, flashing a sharp glance in his direction before slipping into the long grass; a buzzard swept high from the skyline. Raymond Conroy had chosen a suitably deserted area in which to hide himself, Eric considered grimly. The road narrowed, ran deeply between screening hawthorn hedges that had been planted centuries ago, and then he slowed, looking for the ancient drover track to the left that Conroy had warned him about.

The stony way was narrow, rutted and unkempt, and the ditch to one side was rank with long grass and sedge and strangling weeds. The surface was potholed, gravelly and uneven: the Toyota lurched from side to side, clanking and scraping metalled complaints as he slowed to avoid the worst of the holes. He followed the track for half a mile and finally made out the narrow, dilapidated stone bridge he had been advised to negotiate. It was now little more than a cart track, an ancient drover's run, he guessed, leading to Rowland's Farm, and probably continuing thereafter high into the Northumberland fells.

When he caught his first glimpse of the farm it was clear to him that it had been disused for years as a working concern: the adjoining fields were rank and overgrown, the farm buildings had a seedy, uncared-for appearance, the cobbles in the yard were weedy and grass-ridden, and the first two outbuildings he passed beyond the bridge, stone-built barns, gaped roofless at the sky. The long afternoon shadows gave them a mournful, unhappy appearance, and the yard was empty of animals: no scratching chickens, no sheep in the field beyond the farmhouse, no sign of cattle. No sign of life.

A disused farm way off the beaten track. No wonder Raymond Conroy had managed to avoid the police searches to date. After the attack outside the hotel he had moved to a rented house but must have still felt insecure. No doubt he would have rented this place in the back of beyond under an assumed name. From the state of the place its owner would have been only too grateful to get it off his hands for a while, he thought.

Eric parked the car near what once would have served as a small kitchen garden. It was covered in couch grass and thistles. He looked about him. The farmhouse itself was typical of the area: stone-roofed, square-built, solid, unpretentious, fit for purpose. But now dilapidated. There were gaps in the end gable of the roof, and no twist of smoke curled from the chimneys; faded curtains hung at the windows, the gate before him hung drunkenly on rusted hinges. The building was flanked by another stone barn, its wooden doors firmly closed, though unbolted, and a low-roofed cow house was located to one side. Both buildings were in similar stages of desuetude.

Eric looked about him at the land rising behind the farm buildings. Beyond the farmhouse itself the bank rose steeply, a gate leading to a field shadowed by tall oak and sycamore trees that would have been planted a century earlier to serve as a windbreak against the winter storms that would come regularly sweeping down from the Cheviots. Even now the sky was darkening, heavy clouds forming on the Cheviot itself, presaging rain. Eric walked forward towards the gate, realizing there was yet another low, stone-roofed building towards the rear of the farmhouse, beyond a crumbling stone wall succumbing to invasive ivy. He saw that there were in fact some signs of recent use: the marks of car tyres scarred the weedy grass leading to the back of the farmhouse. He started to walk towards the wall to look into the yard behind the farmhouse, then changed his mind, turned back, pushed aside the creaking iron-hinged gate and made his way over the broken, weed-strewn path to the front door of the house.

He called out. His voice echoed, sharpened in the empty

195

yard. There was no reply. He called Conroy's name again, and when he got no response he put his hand on the wooden door, lifted the sneck of the latch and pushed the door. It swung open under his hand to expose a dark, narrow, stone-flagged passageway. Eric stood uncertainly in the doorway, not sure whether he should enter. He called again but no reply came. He felt cold at the back of his neck. He glanced back to the empty yard but nothing moved, apart from weeds swaying in a brief breeze rustling across the cobbles. Conroy had said he would meet Eric here: perhaps he had been delayed. Or perhaps he was outside somewhere, hidden, untrusting, watching, making sure that Eric was alone. He had insisted on that over the phone. Just Eric. No police. Only when Eric had agreed did he tell him how to get to Rowland's Farm.

Eric moved forward into the passageway. His steps rang hollowly on the stone flags. The passageway led towards the back of the farmhouse, a dusty staircase leading upstairs to his right. At the end there was a door. It swung open to his touch and he found himself in what would have once served as the kitchen. It was sparsely furnished: a scarred wooden table, two chairs, an ancient rusty fireplace. The fire had not been lit but there were some signs of recent habitation: some dirty plates and cutlery in the stone sink under a dripping tap, a torn blanket lying beside a badly stuffed easy chair with rumpled cushions. The hairs on the back of Eric's neck rose as he heard a faint sound. There was a sudden movement in the far corner, and a scruffy-coated, feral-eyed cat arched its back at him, hissing in fear. When he moved it suddenly shot past him, and it was only then that he became really aware of the fetid atmosphere, the dust-laden smell of decay and disrepair. The grubby, whitewashed walls were peeling with damp but there was something else in his nostrils, a hint of putrefaction. There was something indescribable in a tin bowl under the table: it had been holding the cat's attention before Eric had entered the room.

Raymond Conroy had certainly not hidden himself in luxurious surroundings. Eric turned around slowly; called again. The house made no response other than a creaking, shuffling sound, as though it was gathering into itself defensively, old walls sighing in protest at the newcomer's intrusive presence.

He walked away from the kitchen and back into the passageway. The door to his right again yielded to his touch with a light groan. For a moment he could make out little in the dark interior but there was a sour smell in his nostrils. Again, Eric felt it had been recently occupied: there were two dilapidated easy chairs huddled together in front of an open fireplace, and an ancient, sagging settee. A television set stood in one corner, leaning drunkenly. It had been smashed; there was a litter of plastic and glass on the floor. Eric stepped into the room. The carpet beneath his feet was threadbare. An electric heater stood against the wall. His attention was drawn to the untidy pile of clothing on the settee. He moved towards it, puzzled. He leaned forward and touched soft cloth, picked up the first item under his hand.

It was silk.

For a few moments his mind was blank. Then he realized the clothing had been worn by a woman. A silken dress, stiff in parts, stained. He dropped it, his fingers straying to other items: wispy, expensive underclothing, stockings, panties, also stiff and dry.

Blood. It was dried blood.

Eric took a deep breath. He looked about him once more, his pulse rate rising. The clothing had been thrown down on the settee carelessly, items jumbled together, and lying on the floor he caught sight of a small bag. When he picked it up he realized it was expensively tooled, a crested clasp, a fashionable evening purse. Even before he opened it, Eric could guess what it might contain. He knew he should not touch it, should leave it because it could end up as evidence, but he was drawn to it, almost *persuaded* to open it.

Inside there were items he could have guessed at: the normal paraphernalia of a woman's evening purse. Lipstick, some loose change, eyeliner . . . and a small leather wallet. Eric dropped the purse and opened the wallet. There were two credit cards inside, along with a car park pass card, and some keys. With a churning, cold gut, Eric raised one of the credit cards. In the dim, dirty-curtained light of the room he was able to read the name on the card only with difficulty.

Coleen Chivers.

The blood in his veins was chilled. When Raymond Conroy had rung, asking Eric to meet him here, he had insisted he came alone: no police. Now Eric knew why. Conroy had killed Coleen Chivers. And after he had dumped her body at Tynemouth Priory, he had kept items of her clothing. Trophies. It would have been part of the pattern he had probably employed in the other killings. The women had all been found naked. Their clothing had never been recovered. A shiver ran down his back. He took a deep breath, stood still for several moments then replaced the cards in the purse, put the purse down on the heap of blood-stained clothes and stepped away, back towards the door. He felt the certainty flood over him; it was all so clear now. Raymond Conroy had escaped from his trial at Newcastle Crown Court, had slipped away from the police surveillance, and had coldly planned the recommencement of his career of bestiality. He had found this dilapidated farmhouse as a sanctuary, a safe house, and he had gone back to the coast, prowled the headlands, somehow persuaded Coleen Chivers to come to his car and then he had strangled her, scarred her in the fashion that appealed to his disordered mind. But he must have been disturbed, forced to dump her on the headland at Tynemouth before he could bring her out here to Rowland's Farm as he must have intended.

But he had retained her clothing. Trophies, blood-stained from his attack with his scalpel, his preferred tool of cruelty. He had brought them back here, to the farmhouse, perhaps to gloat over them.

And he had called his former legal representative.

Why? What could Conroy want with Eric Ward? By bringing him here to the farmhouse, Conroy was exposing himself, would be admitting his culpability in the murder of Coleen Chivers. But why would he do that? And where the hell was the man now? A sudden realization struck Eric: how had Conroy got here? There was no sign of a car in the yard outside the farmhouse. The car tracks. . . .

Suddenly, panic struck in Eric's chest. He stepped back into the passageway. There was another door leading off on his left. With a shaking hand, fearful now of what he suspected he might discover, Eric opened the door.

Like the other room, it was a dimly lit interior. But it contained no chairs. Apart from an old oak wardrobe, the only item of furniture in the room was a large bed, pushed close up against the window. It would have been used by Conroy, no doubt, but now there was another form lying still on the bed, half-covered by a disarray of covers. It was a woman. Eric knew that it would be a woman.

And with a sickening sense of dread he could guess who it would be.

Raymond Conroy had drawn him to this farmhouse, the lawyer who had acted for him. And he would have done it for some unknown perverted reason, perhaps merely to get back at the system that had almost incarcerated him. He had drawn Eric Ward here, and he would have drawn Sharon Owen also. Eric had tried to speak to her at her chambers but was informed she had already left. To come here.

Where she had been attacked. Eric stood above the prostrate form of the young woman, numb, unable to move immediately. She was lying on her back, her eyes closed, one arm thrown wide. There was a dark mark on her cheek, a dribble of blood from her nose. He moved closer to her, leaned over her, touched her face, whispered her name.

He suddenly realized there was a movement of her mouth; a sound like a sigh came from her. Her breasts were rising and falling regularly. She was alive! He bent over her, lifted her gently in his arms, called her name but her body lolled helplessly against his. As his face came close to hers he suddenly became aware of an unfamiliar odour. His nose touched her cheek. She had been sedated, roughly; she had struggled, but now she would be unconscious, he guessed, for a little while.

Eric hesitated, uncertain what to do. He glanced wildly around him. Somewhere, he knew, Raymond Conroy would now be waiting, watching, with some unpleasant purpose in mind. Eric could not guess at it. He could not wait to even try. He knew he had to get Sharon out of this death house. He slipped an arm under her body, draped her bare arm around his neck and lifted her, cradling her limp frame against his body. He stepped towards the door, stumbling slightly, lurching against the damp wall.

It was at that moment, as he straightened, that he caught the dim flash of light as the front door was thrown open. He heard movement, steps, as someone came into the stone-flagged passageway.

2

Eric held his breath. It had to be Conroy and the killer would know exactly where Eric was. He would have been watching, waiting. From his hiding place in one of the barns, perhaps, he had seen Eric's car arrive. He would have waited a little while, making sure that no one else was with him. Now he had come for the confrontation he had arranged. Eric gritted his teeth, his heart hammering in his chest as a surge of anger drove through him. He turned, carefully laid Sharon's inert form back on the bed and stepped quietly behind the door. He stood in the shadows of the room, and waited as the steps in the passageway echoed on the stone floor. They stopped outside the room that held Eric and the unconscious Sharon. They stopped, waited, and Eric could hear harsh breathing.

Then the door slowly opened.

The man stood framed in the dimly lit doorway. Eric edged out from the darkness. With a lurch of relief in his chest, he realized the man standing there was not Raymond Conroy: this man was shorter, but even in the dim light, somehow familiar. For a few moments, as they stared at each other, Eric was unable to put a name to the face. Then suddenly he knew who it was.

'Fraser! What are you doing here?'

The man waved a vague hand behind him, half-turned his head. 'I'd arrived a few minutes before you. Then I heard your car. I didn't know who it might be. Thought it might be Conroy. So I got out, put my car under cover. Watched until

I saw it was you.'

'I didn't see your car.'

'Parked it around the back, out of sight. Couldn't take any chances.'

Eric was relieved, but puzzled. 'So where's Conroy? Have you seen him?'

Fraser ignored the question. He looked past Eric, then moved into the room towards the bed. He leaned over Sharon's crumpled form. 'Is she all right?'

'She's unconscious. I think she's been drugged. We need to get her out of here.'

Fraser turned his head to stare at Eric. He was silent for a few moments, thinking, calculating. 'Have you forgotten about Conroy?' He glanced about the room as though searching for something. 'What will happen if he comes back as we're leaving? What if he's out there waiting?'

Something in Fraser's attitude was puzzling Eric. He shook his head, trying to clear it. Everything seemed out of kilter somehow. He put his hand on Fraser's arm. 'How did you get here? How did you know Conroy was hiding out here at the farm?'

'Did you see the female clothing in the other room?' Fraser asked, ignoring the question, stepping away from Eric's restraining hand. 'Trophies. From Coleen Chivers.'

'So ... you've already been inside the farmhouse. This isn't the first time.... You've been here before.' Eric said slowly.

'I've been here.' The journalist pushed past Eric, stepped back into the passageway. 'Have you looked around, searched the rest of the house?'

He seemed oddly uncaring about Sharon. Eric glanced back at her sprawled figure on the bed. It was necessary to get her out of here, but at the same time he was curious.

There was a tingling at the back of his neck; he was confused by Fraser's odd, nervy behaviour. There were questions to which he had no answer.

'Have you looked upstairs yet?' Fraser called to him in a low voice. 'We should check all through the house, don't you think?'

The man was already on the stairs. Reluctantly, but still on edge, Eric followed him. The shaky wooden stairs were uncarpeted and they creaked and groaned as the two men ascended. Eric was forced to duck his head at the top of the stairs because of the low cross beam at the landing but the hallway at the top was wide. Probably a converted loft, he guessed. Fraser was opening one of the two doors which led off the timber-floored landing. He put his shoulder against it. This door opened only with difficulty, groaning a protest. Fraser looked inside then turned back, shaking his head at Eric.

'Empty. Let's look in the other room,' he suggested.

Numbly, Eric did as Fraser suggested. He stepped forward, raised the sneck of the door, pushed against the scarred wood. There was a dry, dusty odour to the darkened room. He looked inside but could see very little: the windows were shuttered. Eric made out some vague outlines, a chair, an overturned stool. He moved towards the window, stumbled over something, then pushed at the old shutters. One of them swung open, allowing light to stream into the room. Dust flecks rose and danced in the air. Eric turned back towards the doorway, and it was then that he saw it, swinging slightly, pendulum-like, with a slight creaking sound from the overhead beam.

The man was completely naked. His skin had an odd greenish tinge. His head hung sideways at an unnatural angle, his tongue forced out between his gaping mouth in a

203

horrifying rictus. His arms were dangling by his side. A dark stain ran down the inside of his thigh, the last protest of his body before death. The rope had been knotted just behind his left ear; the other end of the rope was attached to an exposed, sagging beam in the roof. It had been wound twice around the beam, knotted firmly. To one side of the dead man's foot was the stool Eric had dimly noticed on entering the room: it had been kicked aside, allowing for the drop. The feet of the corpse were just a matter of inches from the floor: this would have been no matter of a broken neck. He would have died of a slow, dancing, kicking strangulation.

Eric stepped closer. He stared at the barely recognizable, twisted features of the dead man.

'Raymond Conroy,' he murmured, stunned.

His mind whirled, questions tumbling around in his head. He turned to stare at his companion. 'What the hell's gone on here?'

There was a short silence. Fraser still stood silently in the doorway, staring at the hanging man. Eric could not make out his features but he seemed calm, almost unmoved. His tone was measured, speculative. 'Justice of a kind, perhaps. A finality he deserved. After all, he was a monster. Perhaps he couldn't face himself any longer. Maybe he came to the end of his tether.' He snickered lightly. 'If you'll excuse the pun.'

Eric frowned, glaring at the journalist. 'What the hell is that supposed to mean?' he snarled, irritated and shocked by the man's insouciance.

Fraser shrugged indifferently. 'Hey, it's only a thought. But he killed those women in the Midlands. Then the Coleen Chivers woman. Maybe it was all too much for him in the end. An insupportable burden of guilt. Perhaps he was finally appalled by his own perversions, felt he had to bring an end to his own savagery. Or maybe he knew he would eventually be caught, wouldn't escape a second time. So he came up here, with the rope and the stool and put an end to it himself. Perhaps he decided he'd rather face the rope by his own hand, rather than a lifetime of incarceration. Who knows? Who will ever know? When I get around to writing about it I could attempt to produce some reason in my account—'

The man was unmoved, obsessive, self-centred. A wave of disgust swept over Eric. 'Sharon,' Eric interrupted. He pushed past him. 'We need to get her out of here.'

Fraser stepped aside reluctantly, allowing Eric to hustle towards the stairs. 'She would probably have been the next victim,' he suggested, nodding thoughtfully. 'He would have enticed her here, as he did you. He would have played with her in the same way as he did the others, carving her before finally strangling her. But probably, at last, his conscience, his feeling of guilt, his admission of responsibility all washed over him. Made him take his own life. Interesting . . . a fascinating psychological twist. . . .'

Eric hurried down the stairs. He re-entered the room Conroy would have used for a bedroom. He was approaching Sharon's inert form when a thought struck him. He glanced back. Fraser had followed him and was now standing in the doorway, one hand stuck casually in the deep pocket of his worn leather jacket. 'You said Conroy enticed Sharon here.'

'That's pretty obvious.' Fraser shrugged carelessly. 'I presume so.'

'But you also said he enticed *me*. How would you know that?'

There was a short silence. Then Fraser chuckled, a light, dry sound in his throat. 'Well, I could say that it was just a

205

good guess, because you're here, after all. The two lawyers
. . . as a theory it still needs a little working on, I suppose.'
He chuckled again. 'But I suppose it's time to forget
charades like that.' He stood a little straighter in the
doorway. 'In fact, it wasn't Conroy who enticed you here at
all. Nor Miss Owen either, for that matter.'

Eric frowned. 'What do you mean? I spoke to Conroy on
the phone. He asked me to come here, to the farm.'

'No. You spoke to *me*.' Fraser shook his head, clucking his
tongue mockingly. 'You must have noticed the strangeness
of the voice. The harshness. The breathlessness. The
unreality of it. It's strange, isn't it? An urgency injected into
the tone, the muffling of a handkerchief, announcing myself
as Conroy . . . it was enough to fool you both. I told Miss
Owen you were already here: she came running. And you
were easily persuaded too. What was it? Bad conscience,
that you'd let a murderer escape? No matter. Two simple
phone calls. Brought you both here.'

Eric straightened, the blood beginning to pound in his
head. 'What the hell is this all about?'

Fraser seemed to hesitate for a few moments, thinking.
Then he took his hand out of his jacket pocket. Eric caught a
glimpse of something dark, glinting dully in the dim light. A
handgun. Fraser waved it in his direction, almost casually.
'Did I ever tell you I'd spent some time in prison? I think I
did. Prison is supposed to rehabilitate you. But in fact it
teaches you new tricks. You pick up all sorts of information
while you're inside, develop all sorts of skills that are denied
to you in the outside world. Like faking a man's voice. And
knowing where to get hold of a dangerous weapon like this.'

Eric stared at him, bemused. Behind him, on the bed, he
heard Sharon stir a little, murmur something then lapse
again into unconsciousness. The gun muzzle was now

206

pointing, unwavering, directly at Eric.

'Raymond Conroy, upstairs,' Eric said slowly, struggling to piece things together. 'Was it really suicide?'

'No, no, of course not,' Fraser replied easily. 'He died early yesterday, but it was quite a subdued affair. And it was time anyway. He'd given me all the information I needed; he was getting a bit suspicious, as a matter of fact, answering all my questions. And then there was the television report. He kicked in the set when he heard the police were after him for the murder of Coleen Chivers. So I had to speed things up a bit. Which I thought might raise a slight problem, forensically. After all, he couldn't die too long before Sharon Owen, if my scenario was to hold water. There's a deep freezer in the shed outside, and that helped a bit, but I couldn't allow the deaths to be too far apart, forensic science being what it is these days. No, he was quiet after I drugged him . . . another little skill I picked up in prison . . . and then he died really without knowing too much about it. Though I have to admit, I found it a bit of a struggle getting him up the stairs. And strung up on that beam.'

A cold chill seemed to have struck Eric. He glared at Fraser, still not understanding. 'You killed him . . . and you said . . . you implied Sharon has to die.'

'That's right,' Fraser said confidently. 'Oh, I'll dress it up a bit, using a knife, the way Conroy was accustomed to, but she won't feel the blade. She'll be unconscious before I strangle her. That's the way Conroy always did it, isn't it? He worked on them with the scalpel, did his designs, then strangled them. Zodiac designs.' He grunted contemptuously, then laughed. 'I had a design too. A different design. Design for murder.'

'So you killed Coleen Chivers?' Eric asked slowly.

'That's right. She wasn't a Conroy victim,' Fraser

admitted. 'But I'd made sure there were sufficient similarities with the Zodiac killings to have the police chasing after him. They jumped quickly to the conclusions I'd intended. And when Sharon dies in the same manner, shortly, they'll follow the same trail and it will be put down to him. The women in the Midlands, Coleen Chivers, and finally Sharon Owen – the police will assume he killed them all before he topped himself.'

'And me?' Eric asked grimly.

Fraser waved the pistol. 'Well, I'm forced to admit that it's not a *perfect* scenario. But it goes like this. Sharon Owen came to this farmhouse after a phone call from Conroy. So did you. The Zodiac Killer was at the end of his tether, he had decided he was going out in a blaze of glory. He strangled Sharon just before you arrived, had started using the knife on her. But when he heard your car he waited until you came in and then he used a gun . . . *this* gun . . . on you. After which he played out the game as he'd planned. Until finally, remorseful, he went upstairs and hanged himself.'

'That's crazy! You'll never get away with it! Why would Conroy feel remorse like that? And forensics will be able to determine the timing of the deaths. They'll realize Conroy must have died before Sharon or me!'

Fraser ducked his head, and smiled. 'Oh, I don't think so. It'll be some time before the police trace Conroy to this cottage. I'll send them an anonymous tip, probably in a few weeks' time. By that time it will be virtually impossible for them to reach such specific conclusions. They might have doubts, but there'll be no real evidence to lead them to what actually happened.'

There was a short silence. Fraser regarded Eric with a certain cynicism in his smile. 'Go on,' he urged. 'Point out what other weaknesses there might be in my scenario.'

It was a wild scheme, but it could work, Eric concluded. And even if the police had doubts, how would they be able to link Fraser to all this? He himself was still in a daze as to Fraser's motivations. Slowly, he said, 'Why are you doing all this? You wanted to find Conroy, you came to seek my help at the time. What is this all about? Just to write those damned articles in the press? Is that all that's behind this madness?'

Fraser laughed. 'Well, you must accept the articles have been well received, and yes, I hope to write a book eventually, getting inside the head of a murderer. And who will be able to gainsay my theories? Not Conroy. And not you or Sharon. You'll have nothing to say to add to the facts from your grave.'

'I can't believe you've killed two people, and are thinking of killing me and Sharon,' Eric exploded, 'merely to be able to write a series of articles, or a book about Conroy!'

'It will give me credit,' Fraser replied calmly. 'I've been struggling at the bottom of the heap all these years. I know I've got talent, but it's been unrecognized. Now it will be seen, accepted . . . oh, yes, I expect to make money out of this. And gain satisfaction, the respect I believe I deserve, after dragging myself up by the bootstraps all these years.'

'I can't believe it,' Eric said slowly. While he kept Fraser talking, he thought, there might come a moment when the man's guard would relax, when the tables could be turned. 'I can't believe that on such flimsy excuses. . . .'

Fraser raised the gun menacingly. 'Not so flimsy, Ward! You don't know what I've been through, seeing other people wealthy, successful. . . .' There was a snarl in his tone as he took a step forward into the room. Then he seemed to take a grip on his emotions and his voice softened, became more reasonable. 'But, you're right. I should admit it to you: I've always seen, since the trial of Raymond Conroy, that this could be the route for me, leading to success in journalism. It became part of my design, my design for revenge and murder. It's why I came to see you at your office. You turned me away, but I saw Conroy arriving to meet you at the Quayside. I followed him, kept an eye on him until the police attentions became too irritating. Then I approached him, made the proposition. I told him I'd find a safe house for him – under an assumed name – in return for his life story. He never intended telling me the truth, of course, nor did I expect him to do so, but it brought him here, to Rowland's Farm. And I got some material for my writing.' He paused, his voice hardening. 'But you're right, the writing, it's not the only reason. In fact, it was never the main reason. No, the main reason is rooted way back in the past.' He gestured towards Sharon, still lying unconscious on the bed. 'You must know what these two women had in common: Miss Owen and Coleen Chivers.'

Eric hesitated. 'They were cousins.'

'Ah, yes,' Fraser agreed, 'but something else too. They were living a good life, wealthy, successful . . . and I was not. Do you know why that was the case, Ward?'

'The exigencies of life,' Eric replied through gritted teeth.

'Ah, *exigencies*, a good word. I must work it into my next article on the madman who was Conroy. But what did those exigencies involve? The two women, they had privileged backgrounds. They were brought up in middle-class homes; they had money behind them; they were able to become successful in their own right, as individuals, because they had had a good start, had money behind them. Money, privilege, secure childhoods . . . *background*. Things that were always denied me.'

'That happens,' Eric replied coldly. 'Backgrounds differ.'

Fraser waved the gun and grunted in contempt. 'Ah, no doubt you're about to tell me you came from an underprivileged background yourself, that you made your own way in life, that you succeeded against overwhelming odds. But don't waste what breath is left to you, Ward. You don't understand what I mean. Sharon Owen, and Coleen Chivers, they had the advantage of money and background; I did not. Never have. But I *should* have had at least some of what they had!'

'And why should . . .'

'Why should I expect it?' Fraser laughed harshly. 'Why? Because these women and I did share something, if not the money.' He paused, and the gun muzzle wavered slightly as he took a deep, dissatisfied breath. 'Because we all three shared the same blood! But while they gained by it, I did not!'

3

The farmhouse was an old one in a decayed condition. There would always be creaks and groans from the woodwork, the storm-battered roof, the worm-eaten walls. Perhaps the wind had risen in the valley: there had been storm clouds building above the Cheviot hills. But Eric thought he had caught a slight sound from the yard outside. Fraser seemed not to have noticed, as he talked about himself and his anger rose. But Eric's mind flitted away from the thoughts of sounds outside as the statement Fraser had uttered ground its way into his consciousness. It was several seconds before he could get out the words.

'You and Sharon are related? You, Coleen and Sharon are . . . *cousins*?'

Fraser seemed irritated. 'No, no, you're not listening! Sharon and Coleen were cousins, of course. But you're a generation adrift. My relations were Peter and Anne Chivers. They shared a father with me, if not a mother. I was their half-brother. The one they all refused to recognize.' He bared his teeth mirthlessly. 'I'm merely the wicked *uncle* to the two young ladies.'

Eric was silent, his mind spinning.

'Oh yes, the forgotten, unknown and now utterly wicked uncle.' Fraser took a deep, satisfied breath. 'That's what this was all about, really, not the *journalism*, for God's sake. That was only a satisfactory by-product. No, it was all about revenge, putting right an old wrong from years ago.'

Eric was puzzled for a moment, then his thoughts slipped back to conversations, with Strudmore, Sharon herself and the civil servant Linwood Forster. Quietly, he said, 'George Chivers.'

Fraser's head came up, as though he was surprised. 'So you know my father's name! Old George, the licentious, devious, lying bastard. Ah, yes, of course, you would have been involved with administration of the Chivers Trust, perhaps?' He nodded. 'Yes, that would be it . . . The *fons et origo* of all the Chivers wealth, old George. At least, as far as the selected few of his family were concerned.'

Eric stayed very still. The pistol in Fraser's hand still menaced him. His mouth was dry. 'You say George Chivers fathered you as well as Peter and Anne, but I've seen the papers for the Chivers Trust. Your name hasn't appeared—'

'That's the whole point, surely! Wrong side of the blanket,' Fraser muttered viciously. 'You clearly don't know the whole story. But then, why should you? Coleen and Sharon didn't know either. Love, lust, betrayal. . . .'

Eric's mind was beginning to function clearly again.

'Scotland. This is about what happened in Scotland in the seventies, nearly forty years ago.'

'Precisely.' Fraser was silent for a little while as the house still creaked and groaned about them. 'It all seems so pointless now, but there was the Cold War and international tensions. There was a lot of trouble about in those days. The siting of the nuclear submarines, the Polaris, the bloody government kow-towing to the Americans. And they placed the missiles near a city, for God's sake. There were outraged demonstrations. My mother was one of the protesters. Sally Chalmers, twenty-two years of age. Naïve. A political innocent. An idealist. Out to save the world from nuclear destruction! What a gullible, misled fool! And what an idiot to be taken in by George Chivers! He was thirty years older than she was, but he got involved, got to know her, infiltrated her Marxist group, passed information back to his masters in London, played the big hero, and she was stupid enough to fall in love with him. He crawled into her bed to tease out group secrets, and when he got the information he needed, he turned her and the rest of the cell over to MI5. She served a prison sentence, not least because she was unrepentant, shouting her head off in court with the others about the iniquities of government policies. But at the time she didn't know it was he who had betrayed her – and she was carrying his child.' Fraser's breathing rasped in the stale air of the bedroom. 'His child. *Me.*'

Eric moved slowly, put one hand against the wall. The gun muzzle came up again, almost casually.

'She never really recovered from her time in prison,' Fraser continued. 'She was released early, because she was pregnant, and because she was ill. In fact, my only vague memories of her are about how ill she always was. I was born and we lived in a tiny tenement room in Glasgow. It was damp, she had no money, and old George was long gone from the area. My mother had finally come around to the truth, of course, but at first her pride wouldn't allow her to seek him out, even though we had no money. Until she heard her former lover had died. Even then, I don't think she would have done anything about it, except for me, the conditions in which we were living, her illness. So finally, she wrote to George's widow. The doughty Flora. The old bitch!'

Eric could guess what would have happened. The letter remaining in the file gave the clue to the sad end of the whole business. Flora Chivers refusing to accept the stigma of her husband's behaviour, drawing a line under the whole matter. Denying the fact of her husband's relationship with Sally Chalmers. Denying the existence of a child fathered out of wedlock by her husband. Threatening a lawsuit if Sally Chalmers persisted.

Denying everything.

There was a harsh bitterness in Fraser's tone now. 'She threatened to put the police on us. She refused to do anything for us. So we lived on in that bloody tenement, and within a year my mother was dead. Pneumonia, they said. I wouldn't know. Because by then I'd been taken into care. And after that there was the so familiar, dreary history that seems to have happened so often in those days. Local authority institutions, uncaring foster parents, physical, verbal and even sexual abuse, running wild in the back streets, a bit of shoplifting. You must be aware, a lawyer like you, aware of the spiralling downwards that can occur.' Fraser's voice shook slightly, still scarred with the memories. 'But it was during the three-year stretch that I did in prison that I finally saw sense. There were educational programmes. I decided I was going to change, pull myself out of the mud, find work as a journalist . . . and one day, get revenge.'

He laughed bitterly; the sound echoed into the passageway, bouncing off the damp stone walls of the farmhouse. 'But you know, even then I was naïve. I tried for various jobs but they were all leading to a dead end. Until I ended up doing part-time work here in the north-east, still getting nowhere, just scraping by. But I did the research in the archives, did the genealogical bit, learned my half-siblings were both dead, found out about my two nieces. And I saw how Coleen Chivers was lording it around with money supplied by her father and grandfather, making a success of her life, living well, wealthy . . . and Sharon here, well, it was clear that she too was making her way in the world. A career at the bar. Something maybe I could have done if I'd had their background, if I'd had what was due to me; as I could have done if George had only recognized me, accepted me as his son, looked after my mother! As I could have done if that old bitch Flora hadn't turned her stiff, hateful back on what her husband had been responsible for!' The words came out in a vicious hiss. 'Revenge, that's what I decided upon. Revenge . . . and in addition, a great story to tell, maybe. Raymond Conroy. Inside the mind of a serial killer!'

Eric knew the man had almost talked himself out. Fraser had felt the need to explain, gloat over the successful achievement of his aims. 'You'll never get away with this, Fraser,' he said quietly.

The man with the gun snickered. 'Well, you won't be around to know one way or the other!'

There had been a slight noise in the passageway. Eric knew it a moment before Fraser also caught the faint sound. The man was turning his head, the gun raised in his hand just as the bedroom door exploded inward, striking him on the shoulder, sending him staggering to one side. There was a snapping sound, an echoing roar from the pistol, but Eric was hurling himself at Fraser and the bullet was buried somewhere above them in the ceiling. Everything was suddenly a noisy, confused whirling blur, bodies tumbling to the dingy carpet, arms and legs twisting, a sharp pain in Eric's forehead as an elbow struck him on the temple, a dizzying, wavering line of sight, until he felt himself pushed aside, lying on his back, dizzy, struggling hazily to get up.

He became aware of Fraser, features contorted with fury and panic, lying on his back, arms spread-eagled. Perched above him, knees bearing down upon the man's biceps, Eric made out the hunched, familiar outline. The panting figure of Jackie Parton. The ex-jockey's face was bloodied, dark streaks running from his mouth and nose, but he was grinning.

'Always did enjoy a rough-house,' he grunted happily, 'ever since the time I got done over at Newcastle Races that day, after the fourth race.'

Then he looked down at the twisted features of the man underneath him, raised his right arm and smashed his closed fist into Tony Fraser's face. The sound of the crunching of cartilage and the spray of blood brought a surge of bile to Eric Ward's throat.

Jackie Parton was grinning. He was in his element.

4

'When you bugger things up, you really do it in style, don't you, Spate?'

Detective Chief Inspector Charlie Spate said nothing.

The afternoon sun sent a narrow beam of light across the patterned carpet of the ACC's office. Charlie kept his eye fixed on that streak of light. He knew ACC Charteris was scowling at him, and Charlie had the impression there would be not just anger but a certain malicious pleasure lighting up the man's eyes. 'So,' Charteris went on, 'I've read your report and if I put it together with what we already had, things would seem to have proceeded something like this. Raymond Conroy got off his murder charge but didn't like the heat we were putting on him so accepted an offer from this character Tony Fraser, the deal being Fraser would find him somewhere to hole up, and in return Conroy would give him his so-called life story, for Fraser to publish. Denying the murders, of course.'

'Yes, sir,' Charlie replied woodenly. He knew Charteris would spin this out, to dig in the knife, deeper and deeper.

'But it now seems Fraser had an ulterior motive. For personal, family reasons, he intended killing Coleen Chivers but making it appear the crime had been committed by Conroy. He then intended moving on to murder his other niece, Sharon Owen, but things got a bit awkward when Conroy found out from television that the Chivers killing was being pinned on him, an innocent man even if he had killed in the Midlands, so Fraser had to get rid of him rather sooner than he'd intended.'

Charlie nodded grimly. 'That's right, sir. He drugged him, strangled him, kept him in a freezer for a short while, then strung him up to make it look like suicide. He—'

'Yes, I've read your report,' Charteris interrupted caustically. 'He'd enticed Coleen Chivers to have a drink with him as she left the evening shindig in the Gosforth Park Hotel by revealing their relationship: in the bar he'd given her a dose of rohypnol, and then took her to his car, strangled her, stripped her, scarred her and dumped her in Tynemouth. All that's in your report. So is the fact that he later rang Owen and this solicitor Ward, pretending to be Conroy – who was dead by now – to draw them to the farm.'

'That's right, sir,' Charlie interrupted, determined to get in his own say. 'He used chloroform on Sharon Owen before Ward arrived. He wanted Ward out of the way as well because he might ask some awkward questions. He—'

'Never mind Ward,' Charteris interrupted snappishly. 'Let's get to the point of all this. I think I'm right in assuming that if it hadn't been for this shady character Jackie Parton arriving at Rowland's Farm to spoil Fraser's party, we wouldn't have got our hands on any of this, would we?'

There was a short silence Charlie was unwilling to break. At last, he admitted, 'No, sir.'

The thin smile on Charteris's mouth held no hint of humour. 'So how come an ex-jockey could find out where Conroy was holed up, when you couldn't?'

Charlie straightened. They were now getting down to brass tacks. He took a deep breath. 'Parton's a local man. He's got contacts all along the river. He's well known and trusted by people who would never talk to us. He made his enquiries, as I'd requested—'

'Yes, I noted that you'd asked Ward to get Parton on the case,' Charteris said, leaning back and narrowing his eyes reflectively. 'But Parton didn't come to you with the information.'

'No, sir, as I said—'

'He doesn't like coppers,' Charteris sneered. 'Putting that on one side, you still haven't explained how he discovered the farm.'

Charlie shrugged. 'He's kept pretty close about that, sir. It was a contact with an estate agency, as far as I can make out

. . . that, and some reports that he received from his network about activity in outlying properties in Northumberland. His contacts keep an eye on such places. The gangs along the river use empty farms like that for storage from time to time. Stolen goods. That sort of thing.' He saw the glare from Charteris, guessing the ACC thought this irrelevant. 'And Fraser's articles raised his suspicion.'

'They didn't raise yours!' Charteris snapped.

Charlie ploughed on doggedly. 'So Parton made some further enquiries and worked out it was Fraser who rented the farm. He took a look at the place, saw Conroy, realized the farm had been rented to hide Conroy there—'

'Smart little fellow,' Charteris observed. 'Gets to the target while we're still stumbling around in the dark.'

Charlie knew he didn't really mean *we*. He opened his mouth to make an angry retort, then thought better of it.

ACC Charteris picked up a pencil and tapped it thoughtfully on the desk. 'So Parton reported back to Ward's office, discovered Ward had gone out to the farm, and Parton himself dashed back there. Just in time.' He paused in reflection. 'Right, let's get all this in clear, straight language. It was you who was responsible for tracking Conroy, and you failed miserably. He vanished on your watch. You were responsible for finding Conroy, and you failed miserably. He died before you even discovered, through someone else, where he had been hiding.'

'Saves the cost of another trial, sir,' Charlie muttered irritably.

'That isn't the point, is it, DCI Spate?' Charteris said icily. 'I repeat. All this happened on your watch, and you failed. And then, finally, you took Fraser into custody, brought him into the cells and questioned him, and he sang like a free-as-the-air bird. And then . . . after that, well, although I've read

219

your report, I'd like to hear about it, from your own lips. Indulge me, Spate . . . indulge me.'

Charlie braced himself. He took a deep breath, raising his chin defiantly. 'We took Fraser to the magistrates court for the preliminary hearing. He was compliant, quiet, we had the cuffs on him. We were expecting no trouble. The hearing proceeded without a word from him. Then we took him out of the building, down the steps and it was then . . .' Charlie swallowed hard. 'It was then that he broke free.'

'He was with you,' Charteris murmured softly, 'and two police constables. Manacled. But he broke *free*.'

Charlie licked his dry lips. 'It was sudden. Unexpected. He kicked one constable on the leg, jerked free and ran out into the street. He didn't get far.'

His voice died away, under Charteris's stern eye. The assistant chief constable twisted his mouth unpleasantly. 'I would disagree, DCI Spate. He got a considerable distance, I would say. All the way to hell!'

'As I said before, sir,' Charlie said, gritting his teeth, 'saved the cost of a trial. Two, in fact.'

'And as I said before, this happened on your watch, Spate! You were the officer responsible, you allowed this killer to escape and . . . what was it? A taxi?'

'Fraser ran out in front of it, sir,' Charlie said doggedly. 'It was as though he didn't see it, or maybe it was deliberate. But he got hit, he smashed his head on the kerb. . . .'

'On your watch. . . .'

Charlie stood stiffly to attention. He'd been expecting this for some days, but Charteris had kept him dangling.

Charteris threw the pencil down, leaned forward, forearms on the desk as he stared at the man standing in front of him. 'This whole thing, this farce, it's been nothing less than a catalogue of disasters, Spate, a long trail of incompetence. You know, ever since you came up here from the Met, where you had already developed a certain reputation for careless and irresponsible behaviour, I've had my doubts. I've kept my eye on you. You've had some success, but in my view it's all been down to blind luck, chance, not good police work. But this business tops the lot. You allowed a killer to escape, failed to find him, and then allowed *his* killer to escape from custody! How incompetent can a copper get? You must know there are other rumours circulating around the force now as well . . . some related to your experiences in the Met, others to your behaviour up here. But this tops the lot. You realize, of course, your suspension will be confirmed. And then there will be an internal enquiry.' He paused, glaring at the man in front of him with a malicious gleam in his eye. 'You've not got many friends up here, Spate.'

Suddenly, Charlie knew what he was going to do. He eased his stiff back and glared at Charteris in contempt. The assistant chief constable guessed what was in Charlie's mind. He nodded, slowly. Perhaps he had even been hoping for it. 'There is another way out of this, of course,' he said quietly.

Charlie nodded in disgust. He'd had enough.

Charteris grimaced. 'You could resign. Seek your fortunes elsewhere. No enquiry. No mud-slinging. No problem about accumulated pension rights.' He paused. 'We might even arrange a certain pay-off.'

'And I'd be out of your hair.'

'Not just mine, Spate. Not just mine.'

Charlie plunged his hand into his jacket pocket, threw his warrant card on the desk of the assistant chief constable. It was as simple as that.

*

Out in the car park Charlie Spate felt as though a weight had been lifted from his shoulders. He sat in the car for a little while, thinking. After leaving Charteris he had cleared his desk rapidly: there was little there that he wanted to take with him. He had been tempted to call into Elaine's office, have a word with her, but somehow there was nothing to say. Things had changed, they hadn't spent time alone together since she had walked from his room that day, and now he was no longer able to gauge his feelings. He had never been able to weigh up hers. Perhaps things were best left as they were. For a while at least.

He drove into Newcastle and parked in Grey Street near the Theatre Royal. He walked down a side street to the King's Head. The bar was almost empty. He ordered a pint of bitter, took it from the silent barman and retreated into a dark corner. There was a handsome, dark-skinned man near the window. Resembled the photograph of George Khan. The lover of Coleen Chivers, still under surveillance of MI5, but cleared of involvement in the death of the Chivers woman. False leads. Charlie shook his head.

As he sipped his beer he was reminded of the hard men who had come up from the Midlands: Nick Capaldi and Gary Lawson had gone back to Birmingham now, and although they'd had no hand in the final demise of Raymond Conroy, they would have been satisfied enough with the outcome. As for Fraser, the two thugs wouldn't have cared about his death either way, Charlie guessed: though they might have applauded the way he'd turned off Conroy, swinging from that beam.

And now Charlie had to think of the future.

Returning south didn't appeal to him. Seeking employment with another force wasn't an option that appealed to him. He thought maybe he'd stick it out a bit longer in the north. Security work. Private enquiries. Office space was cheaper up here than in the Smoke. And villains maybe simpler . . . apart from some of the big ones.

He finished his pint and went back out into Grey Street, then strolled down to the Quayside. The Millennium Bridge was opening its eye to allow a freighter through to dock near the old Customs House. He watched it for a while, then looked back to the second floor of the building where Eric Ward had his office. He turned, made his way to the door and climbed the stairs.

Susie Cartwright was putting on her coat, just about to leave. He caught her eye: she seemed to be about to say something in protest, at the fact he had no appointment, but then thought better of it. She brushed past him and left the office. There was a light on in Ward's room. Charlie tapped on the door, opened it, then walked in without waiting for permission. Eric Ward looked up from the papers scattered on the desk in front of him. His face was still faintly bruised. He said nothing. He didn't even seem surprised.

Charlie took a seat without invitation. The two men stared at each other silently for a little while. Then Charlie said, 'How's Miss Owen?'

'She's recovered well enough. She's a resilient young woman.'

'Nearly got killed.'

'That's right,' Ward agreed solemnly. He seemed to be waiting for something.

'You too.'

'That's right.'

'If it hadn't been for me, you'd never have got away from Rowland's Farm,' Charlie growled.

'Now exactly how do you make that out?' Ward asked calmly.

'Jackie Parton rescued you both from a tight fix. He wouldn't have been able to do that if I hadn't asked you to get him involved.'

The silence grew around them. Eric Ward shrugged. 'I suppose that's one way of looking at things.'

Charlie hesitated. 'I've packed it in. The job, I mean.'

Once again, the solicitor did not seem surprised. He waited.

'So you owe me one,' Charlie suggested. 'Getting Parton involved like that. Saved your neck. And Miss Owen's.' Charlie hunched his shoulders and slid down in his seat. 'So I was thinking. I mean to stay up here. Find an office, take on security work. Do some private enquiry stuff. You use agencies from time to time. You could use me.'

Eric Ward raised an eyebrow. Charlie guessed what he was about to say. They had a history, he and Eric Ward. They'd never got on. And now Charlie was asking for a job. In the tense silence that followed he could almost see the words forming on the solicitor's lips. *A job? Not in a million years.*

Instead, after a little while Eric Ward said quietly, 'Yes. Perhaps I could at that. . . .'